Riyaz took a step toward her.

"I am not a boy. You do not need to speak to me as if you are teaching me shapes and colors." He was so close that she could smell the scent of him. Soap and skin. And something wild beneath that. Her hands were shaking, her heart throbbing, and she couldn't seem to make either one stop.

"You're beautiful," he said in the same way that he had just said all those other things. The same tone. It was not soft. It was not said to flatter. It was an observation, like the many that he had made since they'd met, and somehow, that made it almost more...flattering. Because he didn't lie. And he didn't say things to get a response. At least, not that she'd observed.

"Thank you," she said.

Brianna couldn't remember the last time someone had called her beautiful. If they ever had.

Maisey Yates is a *New York Times* bestselling author of over one hundred romance novels. Whether she's writing strong, hardworking cowboys, dissolute princes or multigenerational family stories, she loves getting lost in fictional worlds. An avid knitter with a dangerous yarn addiction and an aversion to housework, Maisey lives with her husband and three kids in rural Oregon. Check out her website, maiseyyates.com.

Books by Maisey Yates

Harlequin Presents

Crowned for My Royal Baby
The Secret That Shocked Cinderella

The Royal Desert Legacy

Forbidden to the Desert Prince

Pregnant Princesses

Crowned for His Christmas Baby

The Heirs of Liri

His Majesty's Forbidden Temptation
A Bride for the Lost King

Visit the Author Profile page
at Harlequin.com for more titles.

To Nic, for being amazing.

CHAPTER ONE

THE FIRST TIME Sheikh Riyaz al Hadid saw the sunlight in sixteen years, she was standing in it.

Her red hair seemed lit on fire by the pool of golden warmth she stood in, her skin glowing. Her lips were like cherries, her body a fever dream.

It had been as many years since he'd seen a woman as it had been since he'd seen the sun. And now, here they both were.

"This is Brianna Whitman."

Riyaz turned toward his brother, Cairo, who gestured to the woman. The way his brother touched her arm, as if there was a physical familiarity between them, made a monster in Riyaz growl.

Apparently, not just within, for both Cairo and Brianna reacted to the sound.

Thoughts, words, feelings, sounds. All of it was the same to him.

Riyaz had been in the dungeon for sixteen years.

One week ago, Cairo and his men had stormed the palace and freed him, taken down the interlopers who had stolen the throne from their father all those years ago.

It had taken a week for Riyaz to go to the upper floors. Freedom was also a strange and elastic concept to him. He had been free in his mind all this time, but now his body was also free. And there was wide-open space, harsh light, too many sounds. He'd stayed where he could control some of what he saw and heard and felt.

But Cairo had come to see him, every day.

As had doctors. Psychiatrists. And now...this woman.

This woman who Cairo had said would not be seeing him in the dungeon, but Riyaz would have to greet in the throne room.

It was a strange thing, being told what to do. Yes, Riyaz had been a prisoner for many years. But it was strange how he had found ways to forget. The dungeon had become his world. He was not told what to do. He had free run of that world. He was brought food. And there was a guard who took pity on him and brought books. A rotation of them. They did not speak. They did not... Get to know one another, but there was no animosity either. And he would read each new book at least three times before the man traded them out.

He had created a workout facility, found ways to keep his body in shape, so that he would not atrophy during his time in captivity. And yet, there had been long stretches of time when he had forgotten why he was doing anything. There was no future to plan for. There was nothing.

He had never known for sure if Cairo had survived the attack on the palace.

When Cairo had returned, and set Riyaz free, he had asked that his brother show mercy to the guard who had brought him the books.

Time had a new meaning now. And there were tasks. He had spent the first sixteen years of his life in such a fashion. His days had been tightly scheduled. There had been expectations of him. He had learned other languages, had learned about other cultures. He had kept his language skills sharp through reading. He read in Arabic, English, French. Consuming information, stories, had kept him from losing his mind.

At least, entirely.

And now here he was, in the sun. Looking at the most beautiful woman he had ever seen.

That was something that had not been supplied for him.

Women.

Appetites were an interesting thing. One could learn to suppress them. He had done so while living in the dungeon. He had gone from living on a diet of rich, elaborately prepared foods, to eating nothing but the bland, boring foods of a prisoner. The same every day. Just enough to keep him going. Enough to keep him fit. They fed him quantity, especially as he added mass to his body, but variety was not the order of the day.

He had learned not to care. And then there were days when he would be overcome with the desire to eat a cheeseburger. He did not know why a cheeseburger specifically. It was not common fare in his family's household. It was not traditional at all. And yet he had tried it before, and it was something that had stuck with him. And it was the thing that haunted him.

So too with sex.

He had been a teenage boy when he had been thrown in the dungeon, after all. His hormones had been in a heightened state.

At sixteen, he had not yet lain with a woman, but he'd thought about it often.

He had been promised to wed a girl who was often in the palace, though he had imagined he would take lovers prior to that marriage. He had thought of her, when Cairo had come to the dungeon. It was her father that had betrayed them. Dominic Hart.

The first thing he'd said when Cairo had come to collect him was that he wanted Ariel Hart. She would complete the contract that her father had broken. Would restore what had been destroyed.

He had decided that during those nights when he had gone over and over the way that things had fallen apart.

But he did not desire her.

His desire took a generic, lush form, much like the woman in front of him.

And there would be stretches of months where he did not think of his deprivation.

And then there would be nights… Nights when he was so hard it was physical pain. Where he raged at the state of denial he lived in. Denial he had not chosen.

He could respect men who chose to live their lives as monks. Denial of self was not a bad thing, he supposed.

But he had lived in *forced* denial of self for years.

And sometimes he… Sometimes the fury of it all was too much to handle. Though there were other times that there was something glorious in the deprivation. For it made moments others would take for granted sharp. Acute.

This woman was a moment of pure, aching need.

What he wanted to do was send everyone out of the room and pull her into his arms.

But he was very aware of his own strength. Of the fact that he had no finesse. Of the fact that he had nothing but fury and need. And that his brother was touching her.

That his brother made love to this woman.

His brother who'd had all this freedom these many years.

Riyaz was the Sheikh. He had been raised to be all-powerful. He had been raised to be in command.

And had spent sixteen years in command of noth-ing much more than what he did in the dark.

He was back in power now. And yet... Cairo was the one with the knowledge, the means, to rule.

It was a strange reality.

But then, his reality had been strange from the beginning.

"Brianna," he said, tasting her name.

It was sunshine. Lemon and raspberry. Somehow.

It had been years since he had met new people. And then in this last week he had met many.

She was the one who shone above all else.

"It's nice to meet you, Sheikh," she said. "Cairo has told me about your... Your experiences."

She was sweet. Hesitant to say anything that might hurt him. As if there was any way he could be hurt.

"Do not be careful with me," he said. "I despise that. I'm not simple. And I am not fragile. In any regard."

The woman looked at him with something like pity, and it filled him with a blackened rage.

"And what is it you are here to do?" he asked. "Are you here to fix me?"

"I am here to help you... I'm here to help you with manners. Etiquette, and... What I do is complicated. But I'm not a therapist. However, I have had some experiences with being shut away from the world. And having to learn how to fit in. What I found is that many people want help with that. And need it. It is not as unusual as you would think. I help people. I helped him figure out how to change their behavior to get the promotion. To figure out how to have a relationship. To ascend the throne. After years in a dungeon, though, I will confess this is a first."

"What job title is that?"

"I don't really have a title. When people need me they find me."

He suddenly wanted to know everything about her. And he didn't see why he shouldn't.

"How old are you?"

"Oh. I'm… I'm twenty-five."

"Where do you live?"

"New York."

"In a penthouse?"

"It's a… It's a town house."

"How did you afford it?" New York was expensive. He knew that from reading. Unless it wasn't true now. But he imagined that it was. He'd read books spanning many time periods. Many of them were older. So it was difficult to say what was a more modern truth sometimes. He did try to look at and remember the copyright dates. For context.

"It is expensive. I… Cairo bought my home."

He looked at Cairo. "And what is she to you?"

"She's the woman that's going to help you," said Cairo. "That's all you need to know."

"It is not all I need to know," he said. "I wish to know everything."

"I am going to begin to see about your other business," said Cairo. "Brianna is going to care for you. While I'm away."

"You're going to get Ariel Hart."

"Soon. But I'm not quite prepared for her."

"She will pay for what her father did."

"Do you think that is… Productive?" Cairo asked, and yet his brother was not neutral. He could see that. And if *Riyaz* could see that—with his long years lacking in social interaction—then it was painfully obvious.

"I don't care about what is *productive*. I'm not even certain what that means. People use that word to talk about all that they accomplish in a day. Days… Nights… What do they matter when you live in a dungeon with no sunlight? What did they matter when you live in a dungeon without other people? You just survive. In the waves of time."

"Yes. But out here there is the sun. Also people. And there are schedules. Which is where Brianna comes in. And we don't have a lot of time. We need to see you ascended to the throne. We need to let the people know that they are free. I would love to give you endless time to adjust to the world around you, but even if you are acting primarily as a figurehead, we need you in figurehead shape."

It was such a strange thing. His brother moved at an entirely different pace than he did. He wore expensive suits. His hair was cut ruthlessly short. His movements were quick and precise.

Riyaz sometimes did not move at all. He watched.

He observed. He could be fast if the moment demanded it. But he did not see the point of wasting energy. Everything he did had a purpose. That was why he had set up ways to work out in the dungeon. If he was going to move, he was going to build muscle. Strength.

That seemed a reasonable aim. Riyaz had lived a life where he had little. So he had learned to economize.

Clearly, Cairo did not approach life with the same ethos. His brother was excess personified.

Was Brianna one of his excesses?

He growled again.

"What?" Cairo asked.

"I had a thought I did not like."

"You're going to have to not growl."

"Why?"

"People don't expect it."

He looked around, at the glittering opulence of the throne room. At Brianna, who was being given to him as… Some sort of guide. At his brother, who was now leaving. "I have not expected any of the things that have occurred in this last eight days. Why should I make others comfortable by giving them what they expect?"

"Because you're a sheikh. You have to be somewhat expected."

"What is your plan?" Riyaz asked. "Give me something to expect."

"In a month's time I wish to present you to our

people. Riyaz... They have been in captivity as well. Even if not quite so literally. But until we can show you, physically to the public, I don't want to disclose what has occurred. We must move carefully. We must not ever allow anyone to think that we are weak. We cannot invite more unrest. Not after what we have already endured."

"I could fight. If we were attacked."

Cairo looked at him. "I know. But I would rather not have to fight."

Cairo turned to go. "I will be back next week. After which I will be going to Europe to secure Ariel. As instructed."

"Good."

"My wish is only to serve."

His brother gave a small bow, then turned and walked out of the room, leaving him alone with Brianna Whitman. And now he would ask her whatever he wanted. Because Cairo was not here to tell him that he couldn't.

"Is my brother your lover?"

Her face turned a startling shade of pink. "Excuse me?"

"He touches you as a man familiar with your body would."

"Cairo is not... He is not familiar with my body."

But he could see by the way she said his name, and by the way that her cheeks colored even darker, that the idea was not an unpleasant one to her.

This time he made sure to keep the growl inside. "But you would like him to be."

"We're friends. We do not have that sort of relationship."

"Do you have a lover?"

Her lips went tight. "What we're doing is not about me," she said. "It is about you. Shall we go take lunch?"

"I cannot eat this food," he said. "Not every day. It is... Too much. I cannot even fathom it. All day every day, changes in texture, flavor. In addition to all these other things going on. How does one even have a thought with so much...?" He waved a hand. "Everything?"

"Is there something specific I can ask the kitchen to prepare you?"

"Porridge," he said. "And bread. Toasted."

The day that he had been set free from the dungeon he'd had a cheeseburger. After that, he had wanted to return to what he knew. He could manage at least one different thing every day, but the relentlessness of it all... He did not care for it.

"Then that is what you will have."

"And then what?"

"And then... Your training begins."

CHAPTER TWO

BRIANNA TRIED TO catch her breath while she waited for Riyaz to join her in the dining room.

She hadn't been prepared for him. Of course she had come here because Cairo had asked her to. And she would do anything that Cairo asked. And disturbingly, Riyaz seem to have identified that immediately.

Was he her *lover*?

No, Riyaz, but I have spent years fantasizing about it. While he has slept with everything except for me.

Her untouched state was directly down to her feelings about Cairo.

He had rescued her. From her father's crime syndicate when she was fifteen. She had been a near captive. Rapunzel, locked in a tower. And then her father had decided to sell her. To a rival crime lord. He was intent on selling his only daughter into what was essentially human trafficking, and Cairo had been... Somehow adjacent to all of it, which she understood now was part of his working undercover to gain access to the palace in Nazul again. He had rescued her from her father's house one night at a party, after he'd overhead his father talking to a group of men about his plans to essentially sell her to a man he wanted to make his ally. He had gone in search of her, and she could still remember that first time he'd spoken to her.

He wasn't too much older than her, tall and handsome, and she'd thought he had to be a fallen angel.

Your father is planning on selling you.

I know.

She had known, and she'd been…afraid. Desperate to get away. Because she knew what it meant. That she would be losing her freedom, her choice over…everything. She'd been making plans to run away but she hadn't known what she would do when she did.

Come with me.

She'd known it was a risk. That it could be out of the frying pan and into the fire. But she had grown up in a world where she could never trust the adults around her, and in the end, she'd decided it was a risk she'd be willing to take.

The risk had paid off. He had helped her create a new identity, a new life. Had sent her to boarding school, had…

And of course she had fallen in love with him. Over the past decade, it had been unavoidable.

He wasn't what she wanted, though, not really.

He was a man who lived on the edge, a man who traveled all over and who took lovers whenever he wanted. She wanted a simpler life. Something normal. Something like the town house he'd bought her, which she'd always loved because it reminded her of her favorite family sitcoms growing up. Homey wallpaper, a clock in the kitchen, some ivy on the cabinets.

He wasn't the sort of man to want ivy on the kitchen cabinets.

So she loved him, even knowing they would never be together. It wasn't a reasonable love. But it occupied her heart, whether she was a realist about him or not.

He was her friend. He'd bought her house. He'd facilitated her business.

He brought her others to help. Because he dealt in people who were refugees from their old lives.

And she had so successfully navigated that transition herself that it seemed only right that she begin to help others to do the same thing.

What she hadn't counted on, when she had agreed to this, was Riyaz.

When he had walked into the throne room, her heart had jumped up into her throat.

He was terrifying. Broad and bronzed, and well-muscled. His jet-black hair was shoulder length, his gaze piercing. His nose was straight, his mouth grim. He had a dark beard that had been expertly trimmed, allowing her to guess at just how sharp and square his jaw was.

He resembled Cairo in some ways. But Cairo held himself with ruthless sophistication, his wardrobe expertly cut, his body honed with lean muscle.

Riyaz looked like a warrior from another time. He was tall, and broad. He looked like he would be at home holding a sword. And maybe in his other hand, the head of one of his enemies.

There was something feral about him, and why wouldn't there be? He had been captive all these years. How could he not be?

And it was her job to help him. Not… Tremble at the sight of him. And certainly not feel embarrassed that he had so quickly zeroed in on her connection to Cairo. The connection that only ran one way.

"How strange to eat at a table," he said when he walked in and pulled his chair out, sitting down heavily at the head of the table. He was pushed away from it, the chair angled, his legs spread wide. There was something so… Blatant about it. It made her feel jittery.

She had never seen someone who just… Wasn't bound by any sort of rule or sense of manners.

He simply was, and expected the world to shift around him.

"Well, it is sort of difficult to try and hold your food and your utensils and a drink without a table."

"Not impossible."

"Well. We are aiming for a little bit better than not impossible."

She had decided that she ought to have the same thing he did. But she regretted it when the bowl of porridge was brought to her. A small plate with dried fruit and sugar was brought out as well, but Riyaz ignored it. Picking up a triangle of toast and dipping it into the bland meal.

She wrinkled her nose and began to put dates on top of hers.

"You said you came from a similar background to mine. Tell me," he said.

"Part of being in society is to learn to observe the agreements that we all make without ever speaking of them," she said. "One such agreement is that we do not ask terribly personal questions of people we do not know. Particularly not in environments like this. If we were at a dinner of state, you could not ask someone about their trauma. And they would not ask you about your time spent in the dungeon."

"Why not? It is the only thing I've done for the last sixteen years. Therefore it is the only thing I have to comment on."

"Right. But… Many other people do not wish to comment upon things that cause them pain."

"You know what causes me pain? The memories of my parents dying. That is particularly painful. Losing sight of my brother in the throne room, wondering if he had also been cut down, while I was dragged away by ten men. Ten men, that's how many it took to restrain me, even when I was sixteen. I raged for a time. But eventually you learn… You learn that you cannot rage always, even at the things that are not fair, because you must bide your time. You must wait. That's what I've been doing all these years. I made sure my body did not die. I made sure my mind didn't… Well. I cannot say that I am the same man that I was who entered that dungeon. But I did not lose myself entirely."

"I see."

He tilted his head to the side. There was an amusement in his gaze, and she wondered if he might've smiled if he was a different sort of man. "You are curious now. And you want to ask. But you have just chastised me for asking questions, so you won't."

"Fine. How exactly did you do those things?"

"Exercise is very good for the mind and the body. Movement. I made sure that I moved. Also… Reading. I have read hundreds of books. Thousands. There was a guard who would bring them to me. You know what I like about people in books? You see their thoughts. It is all plain. Written out before you. When I look at you, I cannot read your thoughts. So I ask you what they are. I should like to read you. As if you were a book. I should like to see the paragraphs between the words you speak. For I think there are many."

"Maybe," she said. "A fair few. But that is very interesting. What were your favorite books?"

"It depends. I love reading for information, because I could not go outside and see things for myself. But then... Reading stories of action. Espionage. That was good as well."

"Romance?"

He had a strange look on his face. "Sometimes I found that difficult."

Of course. Books about human connection. Human touch. She understood that. She liked the occasional romance novel, but sometimes they were too painful.

Because, according to those books, by all rights, the man who rescued you when you were a child should eventually begin to see you as a woman. Eventually, didn't the guardian want his ward? Lies books had told her.

It hurt her to read about people connecting in a way that she hadn't experienced. Being alone like he was... She imagined it was even worse.

"All right. Well, that is good to know. You like to read. That will give you a lot to talk about. Books make fantastic small talk."

"And the weather," he said. "Which I can see now. So... That will also give me something to talk about."

Except he didn't seem like the kind of man who wanted to talk about the weather, and for a moment, she almost mourned what she was trying to do.

She liked him as he was. He was forthright, and different. Part of the problem with her job was that so much of it involved taking someone different and turning them into something the same.

It was what the people who hired her wanted, or what they needed for a variety of reasons. And Cairo had impressed upon her the importance of the situation. The severity of it all.

She understood.

She was going to do what she was asked.

"We should probably begin to discuss table manners."

"I know them," he said, his expression getting dark.

"Rather than trying to remember what happened in the past, I'm happy to begin with a fresh slate here and now. Sometimes... Sometimes when there are memories that are painful, or a time in your life that is painful, it's difficult to try and think back. I should think that maybe it would be easier for you to simply begin again."

He looked at her skeptically. "All right."

She stood, and moved to the side of her chair. "Why don't you stand. And we'll try having you sit again."

"Why?"

"What you did before was a bit jarring."

He stood, and she was unbearably aware of how small she was next to him. She only came just to his shoulder, and he was so... Broad and imposing. He could end her with one hand if he chose to.

He didn't seem volatile in that way, though. At least, she hoped he wasn't.

She took a step toward him, and his body made a strange sort of motion that reminded her of a horse. A great stallion that you had to approach with care. It made her want to extend her hand slowly and let him get her scent. Maybe offer him a sugar cube.

He's not an animal. He's a man.

And yet she looked at him, and could clearly see both, and she had to wonder how much that was true of every human. And just how much they had all learned to suppress it.

That more elemental side of them.

Because in these few moments she had spent with Riyaz, what she had learned was that he was almost entirely elemental.

"You pull your chair back slowly," she instructed, "and don't try to make a sound with it."

"I do not understand. Why people are always trying to… Silence themselves."

"You're used to being by yourself. And… Well, here there are always many people. So if we all made all the noise we wanted… It might be a problem."

"But I'm the Sheikh. Surely I can have as much of the noise as I want."

"All right. That's… Fair. However. Why don't we learn and then…?"

"You know what I do remember when I look at you? My teacher when I was in the nursery. I am not in the nursery." He took a step toward her. "I am not a boy. You do not need to speak to me as if you are teaching me shapes and colors." He was so close that she could smell the scent of him. Soap and skin. And something wild beneath that. Her hands were shaking, her heart throbbing, and she couldn't seem to make either one stop.

"You're beautiful," he said, in the same way that he had just said all those other things. The same tone. It was not soft, it was not said to flatter. It was an observation, like the many that he had made since they'd met, and somehow, that made it almost more… Flattering. Because he didn't lie. And he didn't say things to get a response. At least, not that she'd observed.

"Thank you," she said.

She couldn't remember the last time someone had called her beautiful. If they ever had.

"Do you know how many years I went without seeing anything beautiful? Not a flower. Not the sun, not the desert. Not a woman. Just gray stone walls, wrought-iron bars. Men in uniform. Perhaps they were beautiful to someone, but not to me. The same food. The same space. Everything is different out here."

"Right. Well. Let's… You sit. But… Softer."

This time, his lips did curve. "I do not know that I possess the ability to do anything softer. But perhaps with more care."

"Maybe," she said.

And she watched as he took his seat. This time, much better.

"You can square your chair up to the table, so that you are sitting facing those who are sitting with you."

"Why did you get the same meal I did?" he asked, taking another bite.

"It seemed polite," she said.

"Why?"

"Because I feel as if you… Did not choose to have porridge so much as you are transitioning into the space. And I thought maybe it would make you feel like I recognize that."

"You worry too much about other people. It doesn't matter to me what you eat."

"Now I know that for next time."

"Will we be taking all of our meals together?"

"For a time, yes."

"And what other lessons will there be?" he pressed.

"It's not really like that. There isn't a lesson plan. I want to make things easier for you. So if there is anything that feels especially difficult, you tell me."

And then he laughed. He looked as surprised by it as she did, but the laughter continued. "You wish for me to tell you if I am uncomfortable?"

"Why is that funny?" she asked.

"I no longer know how to recognize discomfort. Or perhaps… Everything around me makes me uncomfortable. I was comfortable in the dungeon, Brianna." He paused then. And she could see him direct the shift in topics. Watch the change in his expression before he did it, marked and clear. "I like the way your name feels to say. *Brianna*. It is an interesting name."

"Well, I know for certain no one has ever said that to me before."

"I have never said that name."

"Well, I have never said the name Riyaz before being prepared to meet you. So I suppose that is… Something we have in common."

"I do not think that comfort matters here," he said. Abruptly switching back. "How can it? The aim of this is not to make me comfortable, but to restore order to the country. So I do not think we should talk of my comfort."

"You had a plan," she said, trying again. "To keep yourself while you were in the dungeon. You had a way of keeping your mind about you. You had a way of making sure that your body didn't fail you. This is not unlike that. There is a mission here. And it is to get you back on the throne. That is as far as we will go now. It doesn't need to be about all the rest of your years. Just about this moment. About presenting you to the people."

"I'm to be married," he said.

"Right," she said. They had spoken of a woman. While she was standing there, but she supposed she hadn't entirely taken the meaning on board.

"Does this woman know you?" she asked.

"She is a woman who was promised to me back

when we were children. My brother knows where she is. She will honor the agreement."

She fought against the strange feeling. One of being left behind. Cairo was going to come back here and help his brother. If she understood correctly, maybe even be in charge of the military. He wasn't going to continue his life in Europe or the United States. He wasn't going to continue to be part of her life in the way that he always had been. There was a place for him here. There was a place for Riyaz.

And for this woman that was going to marry Riyaz.

Brianna didn't have a place.

She should be used to that. But even so, she fought against the strange feeling of loneliness that threatened to overwhelm her.

"Well, I will prepare you for your marriage also."

CHAPTER THREE

HE WOKE UP the next morning when the cold from the concrete he slept on became too intrusive for him to ignore.

The aches and pains in his body were, for him, the equivalent of a sunrise. It was the way that he greeted the day. It was… It was how he knew he was alive.

He dragged his fingertips along the hash marks he had carved into the wall, part of marking his days, part of keeping control. When he had been thrown into the dungeon, he'd had a choice. Surrender to captivity, or turn the dungeon into a kingdom of one, which he ruled.

He had opted for the latter. Within the walls of his prison, he had been master of all.

Being able to leave when he chose was still a surprise.

He began to walk up the stairs, his body automatically bracing itself. Tensing. For the intensity of the light and the sound.

But what he was not prepared for was the side of

Brianna. Standing very near the top of the stairs, facing away from him. She was wearing a cream-colored dress that fell just above her knee. Her ankles were slim and were a most fascinating shape. Her calves creamy and compelling.

And then there was the way the dress hugged itself over her rear end. Which was a craving that surpassed any for food he'd yet had.

She turned, and that was like the sunrise. "Oh," she said. "Where were you?"

"Sleeping," he said.

"Right. Only… The servant said that you were not in your room."

"I was," he said.

"Oh. I…"

"I was there," he said, gesturing down the stairs.

"That is not your room," she said, "that is a dungeon."

He shrugged. "It was the only place that I slept or did anything for sixteen years. I find that too much change is uncomfortable. I prefer to sleep in a familiar place."

He realized that the expression on her face was one of… Pity.

"Don't look at me like that," he said. "I'm not a small animal that you need to rescue. I have been rescued, in fact."

For a great many years he had fantasized about saving himself. Building up enough strength to rise up against the guards all on his own.

But the issue remained of what he would find past the guards that surrounded the cell. And he knew that would not be so simple.

He had continued to build up strength, but for his own benefit, and not really for a longer-term plan. That was the lesson he had eventually learned. That he had to find a way to live as best he could within an existence he would never have chosen, and not make his will to survive dependent on what might happen in the future. He had learned to take it day by day. And it was how he was taking things now. Even though he had the sense that the people around him were impatient.

"I don't pity you," she said.

But he could see that she was lying. "Don't you?"

"No," she said. "I might have some concerns. Why punish yourself?"

"Imagine having to try and exist in a world…" He changed tactics. "Imagine trying to live in the desert. Out there. Very different, I would think, to New York. To a town house there. Imagine living there. Nothing to shelter you from the elements. Everything is brighter and hotter than what you're used to. Nothing feels the same. That isn't what it's like for me. I have lived here before. I have lived in the world.

"But it has been a very long time. And these things that you seem to think are reasonable and comfortable, they are not reasonable and comfortable to me. I need to take shelter from them. In much the same that you might do if you were out in the desert. You would need to get away from the elements."

"Right. I'm sorry. I realize that what you're doing is for your own comfort. And that it makes sense to you. But we just… What we are working on is appearances."

"Right. So you should not care what I do when no one can see me."

"I find that I do, though. Because I don't want you to be sleeping on a stone floor when there is a perfectly good bed upstairs."

Flames licked at his gut. Lust that took him by surprise.

A bed sounded appealing. If she was in it.

He wondered what she looked like naked. How her body would look uncovered.

Was she pale like that all over?

His references for female nudity were classical artwork. And she reminded him a bit of Renaissance paintings. All red hair and pale skin. He could imagine her being curved in just that way. But would she look at him with need or with pity if he touched her?

He could not stand the latter.

"What is the lesson today?"

"I had thought that we would take breakfast, and then that we might spend some time in the library. There is a very expensive library here."

"Still?" It was one thing that he had not thought to explore, but then… He wondered. Had the palace guard been bringing him books from the palace library all this time? He had been afraid… Afraid that his father's extensive collection of literature had been destroyed. Books were so much his companion that the idea of it had… Had been like another death.

And so even upon his freedom he had not asked about it.

He had not wanted to know the truth.

"Yes," she said. "It's wonderful. I've taken some books from it myself."

"I like this plan."

"Maybe later we'll graduate to watching a movie."

He had not seen a movie since he was a teenager. "I would enjoy that," he said.

"All right. We'll plan that. I can talk to you about some of the movies that have been made since you went into the dungeon."

She wrinkled her nose. "I'm sorry. I feel that that sounded flippant."

"You are all much more upset about my feelings than I am."

"I just don't want to make it sound as if I'm making light of what you've been through."

"I cannot erase those years. They have made me into what I am, for better or worse. I'm not angry about it. I'm not wounded," he said.

"How?"

"Because what I learned was to exist in the moment. Not the past or the future. Or to exist in… Someone else's moment. And that is where books came in."

"I see. Well. Shall we go to breakfast?"

"Yes."

"I hope you don't mind, but I had the chef replace your porridge this morning. I had thought that we could start with something slightly different."

"What is this?" he said when he walked into the dining room. There was a bowl on the table, and it did resemble the porridge he was accustomed to. But it was different. There was fruit on it. And sugar. And there was something like bread next to it, but it was not toast.

"It's oatmeal," she said. "Which is very much like porridge. It's just a different consistency. It has fruit and brown sugar, which is how I like it. And I have given you an American biscuit."

"A biscuit," he said, frowning. "Is that not dessert?"

"No. It is a little bit like a scone. Except also not. I found a recipe, and the staff was all too willing to make this for you."

"I'm not sure I'll like it."

"Neither am I. But you can get toast if you don't like it. Because you are not a prisoner. And this is not a dungeon. And you don't have to take whatever you're served. You are the Sheikh."

She was looking at him expectantly. Hopefully. And so he took his seat, as she had instructed yesterday, and he saw a little flare of pleasure in her eyes.

He wished to make her look like that as often as possible. He took a bite of the oatmeal, and he found it was not dissimilar, though the textures and flavors were stronger because of the addition of the sugar and fruit. But she seemed to be enjoying herself, and even though he wasn't certain if he was, he didn't wish to impact on her happiness.

He decided he liked the biscuit very much. And he did not need to enjoy it just to make her feel better.

"Let us finish this in the library," he said. He had the urge, suddenly, to be in that room, where he had not been since his release.

They left the dining room, and they went down the corridor. One he had not been to since he was a boy. It was very strange. Visiting these rooms.

He had been to the throne room. He had been to the bedroom that he had been given. He had been to the dining room. He had not yet been outside.

He had not gone to explore broadly.

It didn't seem to be the smartest thing.

He had a strange sensation, like he was walking in two different timelines. This present moment, and one years before, when he had been a boy. He had not appreciated books then.

But he had learned to. They had been his only escape. His only window into any other part of the world.

And even though he had told her he did not enjoy romance… It was only that it had made him ache. For companionship, at times. But especially when there was explicit description of physical acts between lovers…

He had read in great detail how a man might please a woman in those books. And how a woman might please a man.

But sometimes it was too easy for him to picture such things. And it overtook him. If there was one thing that made him miserable in captivity, it was longing for the touch of a woman and being denied it.

But long for it he did. And being in proximity to Brianna only made it… That much more keen.

For the first time he stood near a woman whose hands he wanted on his body. And that was a need that surpassed any he had experienced before.

But then she pushed the doors open to the library, and for a moment his thoughts were interrupted. By memory. And by the grandeur of it. Books from floor to ceiling. Their colorful spines turned outward. Ladders were positioned around the room, on tracks so that you could explore all the shelves.

His father had spent hours in here.

And Riyaz had not understood the importance of it.

He did now.

"I cannot believe they didn't destroy it. It seems the sort of thing they might had out of spite."

"I don't know very much about the people who occupied the palace before your brother… Before he took power back. But I have the impression it was a dark time here."

"As funny as it sounds, since I am the one that has lived here all this time, not even I know very much about them. Only the palace guards. I've never even truly understood why the dictator kept me. Unless it was simply… He got something out of keeping me like a dog. Perhaps that's it. Perhaps it is simply that chaining me was even more gratifying than killing me.

"Perhaps it made him feel secure in his power. Or maybe I was being held over someone's head. I don't know. I think Cairo had everyone killed. Not the guard who brought me books, though. I asked for him to spare his life."

"Oh," she said, looking pale.

"Did you think that this was bloodless? A coup never is. And the initial one certainly wasn't."

Tension rose in his chest as he fought against the images of those last moments that he had spent in the palace before being taken to the dungeon.

He didn't wish to think of it.

Of course he didn't. He did not wish to imagine his mother's dying moments. And perhaps this was why he had not explored the palace before.

It brought the past too close to him.

He had not spent all these years living in the past. He had spent his days in the present. Because it was endurable.

These halls were filled with ghosts. He was not accustomed to managing them.

He walked to the first shelf, and took out a book. *"Little Women,"* he said. "I have read this."

"Have you? It's one of my favorites."

"Yes," he agreed. "It is good." He traced his hands over the letters on the cover. It had been years since he'd read it. It was one of the first ones the guard had brought him. He moved over to another place on the shelf. "*Swiss Family Robinson.* I have also read that. *Pride and Prejudice.*" He paused in front of another title. "I do not think my father would've kept this one in his library." He touched the spine. It had been an extremely explicit book about a young woman and a billionaire embarking on a sexual relationship. He had found it instructive. And torturous. He was surprised to see it in the library.

She lifted a brow. "I think everyone read that when it came out."

"Did you?"

She laughed and shook her head. "No. I didn't have any interest. But really, a guard brought that to you?"

"Yes," he said. "It was informative if nothing else."

She laughed. And he had a feeling she only laughed because she hadn't read it, so she didn't actually know what he was talking about.

"Here's one I haven't read," he said. He pulled out a battered copy of a book that had a man with a gun on the cover. One of those spy novels, he imagined. He did not mind those.

It looked like a series, and he took several of them, because he read very quickly, and now there were all these books. And he could choose whatever he liked. He was not bound to whatever he was brought.

He could choose whatever he wanted to, change his mind on a whim. For the first time, the excess of choice seemed like a good thing.

Next to him, Brianna began to climb up the ladder.

He watched her, and he could not deny that he… Felt slightly compelled to look and see if he could catch more of a sight of her legs as she went up.

But then the doors to the library opened with a loud slam, and Brianna gasped, her foot slipping. She tumbled down, and he grabbed hold of her, catching her in his arms as she fell.

She looked up at him, her eyes wide with terror. Frozen. And suddenly, he wasn't there anymore.

Suddenly, it wasn't Brianna's terrified face that he saw. It was his mother.

He pushed her behind him, and rounded on the threat.

His heart was hammering. There was a man there in the doorway. And he growled. Moving forward with extreme swiftness and violence.

"Sheikh Riyaz," the man said, holding his hands up in terror, but Riyaz was not moved.

"How dare you?" he asked.

"My Sheikh," the man said.

He heard another noise, and turned. He saw nothing there.

When he turned again, the cowardly man who

had startled… Who had… He had done something. People were dying. It was pandemonium. It was the end of everything. That man had done it. And there were more of them.

Raging, he grabbed a piece of furniture and flung it to the side. Grabbed a chair and smashed it against the wall.

There would be nowhere for them left to hide when he was through.

He couldn't see clearly. His vision blocked by fury.

He saw a chair, and turned it over. There was no one under there. There was a table, and he flipped that as well.

"Riyaz."

Dimly, he heard a voice. A woman's voice. And he turned toward it, taking her into his arms once more and shielding her. "Riyaz," she said. Slowly. Calmly. "It's me. It's Brianna. And I'm okay. I was startled. But it was an accident."

He growled.

"No," she said. "It's okay. It's okay. This is the library. And you are safe."

"You…"

"I'm safe," she said. "I'm safe."

She put her hands flat on his chest, and it was as if it was a movie, and she had attempted to bring his heart back into motion with a defibrillator. Like he had been electrocuted.

It was Brianna. And he could see her face. Her eyes wide with fear…

She was afraid of him.

"I thought… I saw…"

"I know," she said. "I'm sorry. I was startled, and I fell. I should've held on to the ladder."

"No," he said. He touched her face, and found that her skin was as soft as he'd imagined. "You're okay?"

"Yes."

He moved away from her, conscious of the ever-growing desire inside of him, and of the fact that he… He had lost himself. That had never happened before.

Yes, it has.

Only in sleep. Night terrors, yes. He had those. They had to make sure he had nothing loose in his cell during those times, because he threw things. Because he was dangerous. To himself and anyone who was standing outside the cell, but it was easy for him to understand why that happened. He was lost in those moments between sleep and wakefulness, and it made sense that he didn't have a firm grasp on reality.

But this…

This was something else altogether. If he could do this during the day…

No one would ever be safe around him. There was no question, he had to take Brianna's help, or he would not be safe for those in the palace.

There was also no question, he had to protect her. From him.

"Where's the man?"

"He left," she said softly. "Don't worry about it. Don't worry, we…"

"I could've hurt you."

"But you didn't," she said.

"No," he agreed. But the possibility still remained, and he did not know how she could be so… Sanguine about it.

And he realized… He was just one of the many monsters that she had helped reform. By her own account.

So perhaps there was nothing about this that surprised her at all.

Perhaps they all lost themselves and had moments of insanity. Perhaps she had been held in all of their arms.

He growled.

"Now what?"

"I must make amends," he said, deciding not to tell her the real reason that he had growled.

"You don't need to make amends, Riyaz."

"I should go back to the dungeon for a while."

"You don't need to do that…"

But his decision was made. So he turned and left her standing there. And when he got down into the dungeon, he realized that he had forgotten to bring the books.

CHAPTER FOUR

WELL, THAT HAD been a disaster.

She was still trembling. His fury had been awe-inspiring and terrible to see. It had been so frightening. Pretending that she hadn't been scared had been one of the most difficult things she'd ever done.

But she could see the horror on his face. She hadn't wanted to add to it by showing him he'd scared her.

She took a breath and looked around the destroyed library. And only then did she put her palm to her chest and feel the raging of her heartbeat.

And then…

She thought of how it felt to rest her palms on his chest.

He was so muscular. So strong that she had the feeling he could have dismembered that poor man with his bare hands.

He had certainly looked like he intended to.

The way he had held her against his hot, hard body… He had not intended to hurt her. That much she knew. He wanted to protect her. But she didn't know what he had thought was happening. Or whom he had thought she was.

He's traumatized.

She certainly understood that.

She had grown up in a household filled with criminals. And they certainly hadn't treated others with care.

She had been largely shielded from violence and other unsavory things. But when her father had told her that he was selling her to one of his enemies, that man had told her what he intended to do to her in no uncertain terms. It had been explicit, and tinged with violence.

She had always known that she didn't live in a normal family. In a normal house. And like Riyaz, she had books. Books had told her that there were other kinds of families. But the way that her father cared for her was not love. Books had told her there was something more out there.

And then, like it was a story, a fairy tale, Cairo had rescued her.

All she had wanted, ever since then, was to find a normal life.

Instead, what had she done? She had spent the last decade in love with a man who refused to touch her.

You already know it isn't worth the risk.

She did. She'd decided that a long time ago. She wouldn't ever make a move on him, she kept her fantasies as tame as possible. He was her friend, and they were too different and…

Her phone buzzed in her pocket.

And she had a feeling it was that very man.

She answered. "Yes?"

"I would like a progress report," Cairo said.

"He sleeps in the dungeon and he just destroyed the library."

"Oh. Well, that is not acceptable."

"I'm sorry, Cairo. But he isn't just going to be fine overnight. He's deeply traumatized."

"The psychiatrist said there was nothing wrong with him."

"I think he's remarkably well all things considered. But to say that he isn't affected… That would be ignorant. Foolish. Of course he is." She thought of the way he ate. The way that he limited any sort of sensory input.

"He's very careful with himself. He's quite smart. He knows there's a limit to how far he can push himself. I saw that limit today. Something happened. It triggered… I think it was probably a flashback. He thought that I was in danger and he…"

"He what?" Cairo asked.

"Well, I wouldn't have been surprised if he'd picked me up like he was King Kong and climbed to the top of the library ladder with me. He was ready to kill what he perceived to be a threat to me."

"Were you in any danger?" Cairo's voice sounded sharp.

"No," she said. "I don't need you to rescue me. Riyaz was trying to do just that. I don't think he's dangerous." Intentionally. "I just need time. And I really wouldn't… That woman that you intend to bring back? I wouldn't. Not yet."

"I've nearly arrived at her apartment."

"Stall. Do not bring her back here immediately. Anything could… Disrupt him. For God's sake, wait until he can at least eat something more adventurous than oatmeal."

"If you say so."

"I *do* say so. I absolutely say so."

"All right."

She thought back to just a few days ago. Before she had come here. When Cairo had called her and asked this favor of her. The way that his voice had made her feel. The way that she'd anticipated seeing him.

For some reason, she didn't feel quite that way now.

It was probably because she was still getting over that rush of adrenaline.

Her body couldn't withstand the rush of adrenaline she usually got from speaking to Cairo on top of it.

"I need to go find him. I have to distract him," she said.

"You don't need to do that. Don't push him anymore for the day." But she didn't want to push him. She wanted to check in with him.

"Trust me. You hired me for a reason."

"Because I needed someone who could keep a secret."

"Yes. But also, I assume, because you know that I can help?"

"That too."

"Then trust me."

Now she was going to have to try and get Riyaz out of the dungeon.

She made a decision. Then she realized it was one he might not understand. Given his statements about food. But she wondered. She wondered if he was just still withholding things from himself. She knew that he slept in the dungeon. What was the real reason for that? She knew that the transition from a life as a prisoner to a real life must be very difficult. She understood it, at least in a limited way.

But she decided to go to the kitchen and get cupcakes.

There were some made with spice cake and cream cheese frosting. And some that were chocolate with chocolate frosting.

She grabbed both, and went straight to the dungeon. He wasn't there.

She began to hunt around the palace.

The last place she looked was the throne room. And there he was, standing in the back of the room. Just looking.

"Hello," she said.

"What are you doing here?"

"I was going to ask you the same thing. I didn't expect to see you here."

"You do not know everything, Brianna. I hope you are now humbled."

"Mm. Sadly not." She stared hard at him, daring him to smile. He didn't. "I just gave your brother an update on the situation. And I thought that maybe we should talk."

"Why would you want to talk to me?"

"Well, it's my job to talk to you, Riyaz. Also, you're the only person in the palace that I really know. So if I'm going to talk to somebody, it's all the better that it's you."

The look he gave her was nothing if not suspicious. And she lifted the tray she was holding in her hands aloft. "I have brought you something nice."

"What is it?"

"Cake," she said.

"I don't know that I want it."

"I think you should try it," she said. He was looking at her like she had done something strange, and it suddenly made her feel very silly. She took the opportunity to spin it into a lesson, because then it wouldn't feel quite so…personal. "I think that you should try it because it would be good for you to try something new. I think that you should try it because you might enjoy it. Why are you so afraid of enjoying things?"

His lip curled. "I'm not afraid of anything."

"Of course not. You're a warrior. A mighty king."

"I wasn't *afraid*. In the library. I thought I needed to fight, and I was ready. I am always ready to fight."

"I believe you. I didn't say that you were afraid."

She thought he might be afraid of living life without the parameters of the dungeon. That maybe he was reluctant to believe that he was truly free.

"This is where you... Sit? Or... I guess I don't fully understand the concept of throne rooms. What did your father do in here?"

He looked around the room. "This is where my father would entertain dignitaries. Listen to the plights of our people. Decide on new laws. It was ceremonial, mostly. He enjoyed spending more of his time in the library. He was different than the kings that came before him. More modern. Sometimes I wonder if that is why he was killed."

"In what way?"

"He believed in women's rights. He taught Cairo and I that women were equal. He changed many laws allowing them freedoms. He was ahead of much of the world in human rights in general, as it happens. There was pushback against that. People... People the world over are inherently set in their ways. And they do not like things to change. Yes, there are always agitators looking to progress, but that kind of progress scares the masses."

"And yet, he was happy to make a deal with a man to choose a wife for you."

"Yes. There were still political marriages. My parents' marriage was a political one. But they came to care for each other very much. I think my father saw that as diplomacy, rather than treating a woman as if she were an object."

"Good of him."

"My father was a good man. But he was also a man of his particular station. And that is going to be different to your experience."

"My father was not a good man."

"I have some sense of that."

"My prison was very different from yours. In fact, I didn't fully realize that it was one. I lived in a beautiful house. An estate, really. There were so many beautiful places to play on the grounds. In the gardens. I didn't find it strange that we didn't have children over. That I didn't go to school, rather I had a tutor at home."

"You said my brother rescued you. Sent you to school."

"Yes. He did. He sent me to boarding school. Which was a different experience entirely. I had to learn…"

"Was it difficult to learn?"

"Yes and no. I was immersed in it. Thrown into the deep end of society. As far as a teenage girl went. I was happy in many ways, but intimidated in others. I didn't know how to interact with large groups of children my own age. And we weren't children. So there were politics. I learned to navigate those. Through trial and error. I became very popular."

"Why do you think that is?" he asked.

"Because I'm delightful?"

He pushed away from the wall and began to walk toward her. Caged panther. "No. Why do you think that was? *Really.* Because many people wish they were popular. Many people would love to be. And they spend their entire lives in society observing other human beings, and yet can't fit in. But you did."

"I suppose it's because when you live in a home with a man who has a vile temper, reading the room, the situation, can be a matter of survival."

His expression turned fierce. "Did your father hurt you?"

"Not routinely. But occasionally, I would take a backhand blow to the face. Or just get yelled at. Screamed at. Neither was fun. I learned. I learned because I had to. I learned because it is imperative to learn when you're in those sorts of situations. And so, I guess I transferred that need to read the room into my school experience. And from that, I learned to help other people. People like you and me."

"How many people like you and me are there?"

"More than you would think. People who have lived in abusive homes. Or cults. A person who has been in a controlling marriage for a number of years. There are many reasons that someone might struggle in the world. You're not alone."

"I wouldn't care if I was," he said.

"Of course not. Why should you want connection? Or cake? Have some cake, Riyaz."

He looked at her skeptically.

"Riyaz," she said. "You are skeptical of a treat?"

"In my position, wouldn't you be?"

"Maybe," she said, her heart clenching.

He took a step toward her, moving into a shaft of light.

He was beautiful. He had high cheekbones, and the hollows of his cheeks were sharp. Even with his dark beard covering his jaw she could see that.

He was muscled, extraordinarily so.

All that working out he'd done had paid off.

"We've talked about your books. Tell me about your body."

He lifted a dark brow, and her face went hot. "I mean, tell me about how you work to stay... Oh, come on, you're in amazing shape."

He surprised her. Because all at once, he stopped, and he grinned. Then, he chuckled. "You enjoy my body?"

"I would have to be blind not to notice the sort of shape you're in," she said, feeling properly warm now.

"I see. Well. Pull-ups, sit-ups. There was a stone bench down in the dungeon, and I would lay on my back and lift it with my feet. Plus there are many bodyweight workouts that a person can do. I also lifted the bench. I didn't wish to lose my body *or* my mind. There were many things I had no choice but to let go of. My fitness in either of those arenas was not going to be theirs. Not ever."

"I admire that. Very few people would have the presence of mind to make that determination."

He lifted a brow. "Cake and flattery?"

"I'm hoping that you'll take at least one of them," she said.

"I will consider it."

"I have spice cake. And chocolate."

She could see interest flare in his dark eyes.

"You want chocolate," she said.

"I have not had chocolate in sixteen years."

"Riyaz, you must have chocolate. You absolutely must."

She lifted it up from the tray, and held it out to him.

He took it from her, and she watched as he took a bite. And she was more gratified than she should have been by the growl.

"You aren't supposed to do that, remember?"

"You don't mind," he said.

"No," she said softly. "I don't. I quite enjoy it. But don't tell anyone I said that, because I am supposed to be civilizing you, and you do need to learn to not growl in public spaces."

He finished the cupcake quickly.

And then eyed the tray.

"Have another. They're for you."

He did take another. "Maybe you should consider sleeping in your bed also," she said sweetly.

That was met with another growl. "No. I don't think that I could."

"Why not?"

"How would I know when to wake up?"

"What does that have to do with when you wake up?"

"I know when to wake up when I'm too cold. When my body hurts too badly. That's how I know."

"There are alarm clocks, you know. You don't have to count on being uncomfortable."

"Still. I'm not certain."

"Well, that's the beauty of freedom, Riyaz," she said. "The door will be unlocked. So if you decide that you do not wish to sleep in your bedroom anymore you can always go to the dungeon. Because you're not a prisoner. Not now."

"I appreciate that," he said.

"Good."

"I am prepared to sit here." He looked around the room. "I'm not afraid of those who might oppose me."

"Do you think people will?"

"It is always a possibility. Always. But what can be done to me that has not been already done? I have been a prisoner. And I suppose they could choose to kill me. But it does not frighten me. I had to make my peace with death after the first coup."

"You should never have had to do that."

"Maybe not. But it is the way of things."

"Tell me. Tell me what it was like when you and Cairo were children. Before this happened."

* * *

This beautiful woman was plying him with cupcakes after he had treated her appallingly. He had wanted to protect her, but he could see that he had frightened her. And he did not care for that. And he could not quite figure out if she actually wanted to hear about his childhood, or if this was some exercise of hers. But he found he wanted to tell her either way. Because he had spoken to no one about this, not even Cairo. And there was something tantalizing about it. He did his best not to remember when he was in the dungeon. It was as if he had no past or future when he was in there. Nothing but the present, because it was the only way to get through any of it. If he remembered how happy he had once been, he might go mad. If he thought about how much better life would be if he were out, he would surely go mad.

And so now, as a man with a future that did not include the walls of the dungeon, he decided to allow himself to be a man with the past. With her.

"We had a good life as children. We had lessons. For most of the day. Five days a week. Our father was strict. He did not wish for us to grow up to be entitled or spoiled. He was quite concerned about that. He said many kings fall because they love themselves more than they love their people. He said many kings became corrupt trying to protect only their own interests. He did not wish for that to be so for us. So he taught us, not only the sorts of subjects you expect to learn in school, but to give ourselves over to the service of others. To prize philanthropy. Do not take ourselves so seriously. He was a good father."

"And your mother?"

He tried to picture his mother. Tried to picture her when she was not screaming for help. Looking at him with dark, pleading eyes as they…

"I loved her," he said. He could not bring himself to say more.

She seemed to understand. "What kind of a brother was Cairo? I know him as a… A friend."

"A friend you are in love with."

"Nothing has ever happened between us. And it won't. I know that."

"Do you really know that? Or is that why you're here? Do you hold out hope?"

She began to look uncomfortable.

"No. I'm actually not. I decided that this… This would have to be the last thing that I did for him. Because I can't love him, not like that, not for real. I can't. Not when… Not when I want something else."

"What else?"

"This isn't about me. This is about you."

"And Cairo. Admit that you are curious about him for your own benefit."

"Fine. I am. But after this, I won't be as close to him anymore. He's planning on taking over as the head of your military, after all. It matters to him. A great deal. Your health, your happiness…"

"He got along with my intended much better than I did," said Riyaz. "We used to fight about that a bit. He was my very best friend, until summer, when Ariel would come to visit. She was afraid of me. I can't say that I really blame her. She's two years younger than I am. The same age as Cairo. They got along immediately, and he would abandon me for large portions of the day to run wild with her. My parents thought they would make companionable in-laws. Keep each other occupied while I ruled. I always wondered…"

He had always wondered if Cairo loved her. But they had been boys. Children, and Riyaz had never questioned a dictate of his father's. If his father said that he was supposed to marry Ariel, then he was supposed to marry her.

His father could not be wrong.

He gritted his teeth.

What a harsh blow it had been to find out that his father could be wrong. That he could trust the wrong man.

What a harsh thing to realize that in the final moments of his father's life. It made him no less Riyaz's hero. But it did teach him that his father was human. Very, very human.

And he had died like one.

"Cairo," he said, redirecting his own thoughts. Trying to turn off the images in his head of the bloody throne room. The very room they stood in now.

He could not afford to lose himself. Not with her. Not again.

"He was always a big personality. Always brilliant. Always in trouble."

"And you weren't?"

"No. I was the heir. The heir could not afford that sort of behavior."

"And you just… Knew that. Accepted it?"

"Like I said. I wanted to be like my father. And that was the manner of man he was."

He looked at the tray of cupcakes. He wanted another chocolate one. Except… Looking at her, what he really wanted. What he wanted with all of himself, was her. He might not have tasted chocolate in sixteen years, but he had not tasted her either. And he wondered if she tasted like he thought her name did. Like lemon and raspberries and sunshine.

So he took another cupcake.

Because she had offered it. And that was really why it mattered.

Because of her.

"You should have one," he said.

She looked down at the tray. "I don't have a free hand."

He took the tray from her swiftly, and set it on the throne.

"I imagine that's against some kind of tradition."

"If it is," he said, "then I have forgotten the tradition. Therefore it no longer exists. I am the Sheikh, after all."

"Right."

"Have one," he said.

She didn't make a move. So he set his cupcake down, and selected one for her, holding it out.

She came forward slowly, and she surprised him, not by taking the cupcake from his hand, but by tilting her head and taking a small bite off of it.

The proximity to her mouth caused him to feel an electrified sensation that shot down his spine and radiated out toward his groin.

Desire nearly overwhelmed him. He wished to pull her in his arms and have her on the floor. He wished to...

He saw a spark of something in her eyes. And he remembered what she said about being sensitive. To changes in mood. About the way it had been a survival necessity for her.

And he wondered if she felt this. The change in him. The depth of his desire. His arousal.

Or maybe...

Maybe she just felt her own.

"It's delicious," she whispered.

"Yes," he agreed.

"Thank you."

"You are going to eat the whole thing."

"Well. Not out of your hand."

"Take it," he commanded.

And the way that she obeyed him so beautifully only tightened the desire within him yet more.

She licked the frosting off the top, and he was

held rapt to the movement of her slick pink tongue. She was so beautiful.

It was easy for him to forget about Ariel, even though they were talking about his past. Even though his memories of Cairo were tangled up in memories of her.

He had never wanted her.

He had certainly never loved her.

A good thing. For if he had… She would not know what to do with the man he was now. Because he was not a man who could offer those feelings.

He once had been. He might've even come to love Ariel. Like his parents had come to love one another.

But that part of him had been so neatly excised when the light had gone out from his mother's eyes.

That moment had robbed him of a great many things. Then his captivity even more. But that ability to love. To care. To feel anything half so intensely… It was gone. In many ways, he was grateful, for it had ensured his survival. If he had been left a wailing, grieving boy down in that cell, how would he have ever come out of it? How would he have ever survived? It would not have been possible.

But he did not know what the years had done to Ariel. Her father had betrayed him.

"Ariel's father betrayed mine," he said. Because now that the thought was in his head he wished to speak of it.

"Cairo did explain some of the things to me…

He was supposed to be seeking an alliance with us. Through the marriage. But instead he was paid off by the men who wished to take over the country. Who killed my family. He traded us for money." He paused for a moment. "Some might say she should be punished for the sins of her father."

"And you?"

"I don't know. I haven't decided what I will do when she gets here."

Anger burned in his chest. He wondered if she had known. But then, she had only been fifteen. Perhaps it was foolish to blame her for any of it.

And yet… He found it difficult not to.

"Well. I think… I think you shouldn't consider things like revenge. Not now. Your father was a modern leader. He didn't keep those sorts of blood scores, I imagine."

"A blood score?" he asked.

"I made it up. I thought it sounded somewhat medieval, and a bit intimidating."

"Well. Definitely that."

"Just focus on yourself. Finding herself. That is actually what I'm trying to help you do. I'm not trying to turn you into the leader you never would've been. But the one you would've been if not for all of this. The one you wish to be."

"Thank you."

"Sleep in the bed tonight, Riyaz."

He nodded slowly. Perhaps it was time.

* * *

The roar woke her out of a deep sleep.

It did not sound like a man. It sounded like an animal. And when she began to hear the crashing of furniture, she leaped out of bed without thinking.

Riyaz. She knew that it was him. She knew it was Riyaz having another one of those episodes. PTSD. Flashbacks. Whatever they were.

And she knew that she needed to be the one to go to him. She knew it as sure as she knew anything.

She threw the covers off of her bed, and began to run down the hall.

No one else was coming. They all feared him. She had heard them whispering earlier in the day about the mad Sheikh. Referencing what had happened in the library.

Nobody was confident in his ability to hold it together.

But this… This didn't mean that there was something wrong with him. And she knew that. She knew that. Even if he didn't.

Even if no one else did.

He was traumatized. And that was understandable.

All she needed…

She opened the door to the bedchamber, and found a dresser on its face.

Curtains torn down. The room was in a state, and Riyaz was standing at the center of it, a hollow-eyed warrior who looked remote. Unreachable.

Gone was the man who read books. This was the man who lifted stone benches. This was the man at his most elemental.

This was what he had tried to prevent himself from becoming.

Tonight, the beast had won.

"Riyaz," she said slowly.

He breathed out hard, and reminded her of a spooked stallion, his eyes wild.

And she knew that he still didn't see. Not really.

"Brianna," he said.

He shocked her. He *did* know that it was her.

But then he crossed the space and wrapped his arm around her, drawing her into the room. "They will not touch you," he said.

"There's no one here," she said.

"There was," he said, insistent.

"No," she said. "No one is here. You're safe."

But what she said was lost as he growled. And dragged her deeper into the room, throwing his body in front of hers as he pinned her to the wall.

She wrapped her arms around him, her hands on his chest, and she could feel his heart raging beneath her hands. "Riyaz," she said softly. "Riyaz come back."

She moved her hand slowly over his chest, down to his stomach.

Then moved her hands back up. And gradually, she felt his heart rate begin to slow. "It's okay," she said softly. "It's okay."

And then he turned suddenly, hands bracketed on either side of her face against the wall. She could scarcely breathe.

Her heart was thundering radically. His face was so close to hers. And then she reached up and touched him. "Riyaz."

It was like the fog cleared. Suddenly.

And he came back. And then tension of a different kind began to move between them. He moved one hand around her waist, stroking her up and down the way that she had just done him. He was back now, but he was more feral. More himself in some ways, she thought.

He moved closer, and her eyes fluttered closed, and she forced them open. She wanted to watch this. Whatever might happen next.

You're an idiot. He's a sheikh. He's supposed to marry somebody else. You're supposed to be in love with his brother.

Yes. All great reasons to move away.

This is not what you want. You want a normal life. This could never be normal.

Still. She didn't move away from him. Still. She stood there. At his command. Or maybe it was a different command. One that they were both subject to. One that neither of them could deny.

She didn't know what she expected. Perhaps for him to lean in. Close the distance between them. To claim her mouth with his own. Instead, he touched her face. Dragging calloused fingers along her jawline, his thumb moving over her lip. And then he dropped his hand and stepped back.

"This won't stop," he said.

"I…" For a moment she was confused. For a moment, she didn't understand what he meant. But of course he meant the flashback. But right in that second she had thought that perhaps he'd admitted to the thing between them. The pulse that arced there.

"It will. It'll get better. It will…"

He growled. She flattened herself against the wall. Not because she was afraid of him. But because she was afraid of what she might do.

"No. It will not. There is something broken in me. If Cairo needs me to be a figurehead, then that is well enough. But as to whether or not I can rule…"

"Don't let them take it from you," she said, the words coming out fiercely.

She was shocked by it. By the intensity of what she felt. But it wasn't fair. He was a strong man. A proud man. One who would do everything possible to protect those in his life.

Those that he cared for.

He would do the same for his country, she knew it.

"It's PTSD, Riyaz. Soldiers get it when they go to war. Many people have it after they've experienced abuse."

"I read, remember? I'm familiar. But whatever you call it, it is unacceptable for a man like me. For a man in my position. I must be what they need me to be."

"It's you," she said. "They need you. They need you to have survived. And you did. That's what you did for them. That's what you did for the country. You don't have to be perfect. No one would expect that."

"It would be nice if I wasn't a danger to others."

"You didn't hurt me. Did you?"

"You know what I want to do to you?" he said, his voice a low growl. "I want to strip you naked and have you on that bed."

Heat rose up inside of her, and her heartbeat sped up. She could see it. That gruff declaration. His body over hers as he…

She swallowed hard. "That's the adrenaline."

"It isn't."

"You need to go to sleep, Riyaz."

"It will not be here."

"You don't need to punish yourself for perceived transgression…"

"You don't know what I need. If you did, then this wouldn't have happened."

And then he turned and stormed out of the room, leaving her standing there surrounded by the shattered remains of all of the furniture. She was going to have to give Cairo an update.

And if she left out the fact that Riyaz made her pulse race, the fact that his dark, sensual promise did not scare her, but rather ignited in her a need that she could scarcely explain…

That was understandable.

* * *

The dungeon was dark. And it was familiar. And after all of that it was… The right place for him to be.

His pulse was still racing. His mind filled with images of what he'd seen.

His mother.

Always his mother.

Fear and blood and death.

He growled, and he picked up the stone bench, lifting it, and then, he did something he had not done before. He threw it. And it cracked into pieces. The sound of it deafening. Good. He wanted to destroy everything. And that was the worst of it. Coming back to the present moment hadn't stopped that. What he wasn't certain was how he had prevented himself from…

All he had wanted to do was to rip the clothes away from her body and satisfy himself. As if the only way that he could possibly be free of the beast growling through his body was to claim her. Take her. Slake his lust on her.

No.

He lay down in the corner of the dungeon. And he welcomed the bite of the rocks against his skin.

He deserved to be punished for just that thought alone.

And he knew that it didn't matter what she had said. But the door was open.

A part of him would always be locked in here.

CHAPTER FIVE

"No. There hasn't really been more progress. I wish that I could say there was. I wish… I'm sorry. But I'm still not entirely sure what he thinks he's going to do with Ariel. He doesn't seem to know."

"I'm keeping her. Until you do know."

She thought of the way that Riyaz had talked about Ariel, and Cairo's relationship with her. "She's your friend. Isn't she?"

"I… Yes," said Cairo.

"Riyaz was talking to me a little bit about your childhood. About your connection with her."

"I didn't realize he noticed."

"I think he was jealous," she said.

"Really?"

"Of her. Not of you. He said you were always his best friend until she came to visit."

"That's not how I remember it. I remember him being very busy with matters of the state."

"Well, maybe that's something you should talk to him about."

There was a slight pause. "You seem to get a lot out of him. Considering you've made it sound as if he's barely civilized."

"He *is* only barely civilized," she said. "That doesn't mean you can't talk to him. You can. He likes to talk. When you think about it, it makes sense. He hasn't had anyone to talk to for quite some time."

"I guess not. But then… I'm not sure I have either."

Well, you had me.

But she didn't say that.

"I'll keep you posted. I haven't seen him today. I think he's gone back to the dungeon. Regression is somewhat expected. Two steps forward, one step back."

It was expected, but she didn't like it. And she was trying to figure out a way to… To fix it. But she was still turning over everything that had happened. The way it had made her feel. She wasn't afraid of him. That was the thing.

If anything, she was afraid of herself.

She hung up the phone, and took a sharp breath. If Riyaz was down in the dungeon. Then she would meet him there. And she wasn't going to let fear stop her.

She traversed the corridor, and took the spiral staircase down to the dungeon.

She had a blanket. And her tablet. And she had a feeling that what she was doing was possibly foolish. She also had his stack of books.

A picnic basket with food.

When she got down there, she heard a noise. Movement. Masculine grunting.

She froze for a moment, but then continued to walk forward. She went into the cell, but she didn't see him.

Then she continued deeper, and stopped. He was hanging, suspended from a bar at the middle of the low-ceilinged room.

Pulling himself up, then dropping slowly, exhibiting an intense amount of control.

He had taken his shirt off, and was wearing only a pair of black shorts. She was struck absolutely motionless by the sight of all those muscles at play.

He was a work of art. He transcended the strength of any normal human man.

The dark hair on his chest captured her attention, as did the ripple of his muscles.

And she felt something shamefully feminine begin to rise up inside of her. Need. Desire.

What was wrong with her? She was supposed to be helping him. She was… She was supposed to be in love with Cairo. Was she simply transferring her affection because she was near his brother?

She looked at Riyaz, at the way his dark hair fell into his face, and his animalistic movements.

He was nothing like Cairo.

She couldn't hide behind that. Couldn't use it as an excuse.

And suddenly, he looked up and saw her, dark, furious eyes meeting with hers.

He released his hold on the bar, and dropped back down to earth. "What are you doing here?"

His body glistened, sweat rolling down his pectoral muscles, down over his abs. He looked at her, his gaze moving slowly over her body, and she felt a pulse between her thighs begin to quicken. What was wrong with her?

She had been in love with Cairo for a decade, but she hadn't felt it… *There*. Not like this.

"I brought you food. And a blanket. And a movie. And your books."

"You shouldn't have come here."

"You didn't tell me not to."

"And if I had, Brianna?"

"I would've come anyway. Because somebody needed to check on you."

"I've spent sixteen years by myself. Nobody *checked* on me. I'm not a child. And I am not a dog."

"I know," she said. "I didn't say you were. I'm… I'm sorry I…"

"What movie?"

"Well, it's a… It's an adaptation of *Little Women*. I thought you might enjoy it."

"Maybe," he said.

He was looking at her out of the corner of his dark eyes. The suspicion there pronounced. It would've almost been funny if any of this were funny.

All she had ever wanted was to be normal. She just wasn't.

This was not normal.

She carefully set her items down, grabbed the blanket, and spread it out on the square stones. She took her tablet, and set it up. "Have a seat," she said.

He growled. "You growl too much," she said.

"You *make* me growl too much." But he sat down beside her.

He was sweaty, and she felt like she should object. But he smelled… Something was wrong with her. Because she wanted to bury her face in his chest and get even more of the scent of him.

Pheromones.

She dimly remembered hearing people talk about that before. That's what this was. Perhaps this wasn't specific at all. Maybe it was simply that she had left the whole virginity thing too late.

That was Cairo's fault.

She'd been so wrapped up in him that she had sort of forgotten to pursue other relationships. And maybe now she had hit some kind of wall with her sexual dry spell.

It had been fine up until this point, and now it was too much.

So a sweaty, shirtless, muscular man tested the bonds of her better judgment.

Nothing was going to happen. She was *helping* Riyaz. That was all.

She leaned forward, pushing a few buttons on her tablet, and getting the film started while she began to unpack the food. She really wished that she had gone to change. Sitting on the blanket in this dress, which had ridden up mid-thigh, while he sat there half-naked… It was too much.

And she was going to do her level best to pretend that it was not too much, because the whole thing was just…

"Cheese," she said. "And fruit."

"No cheeseburger?" he asked.

"Sorry. I can make sure that there is one for your dinner."

"You act like my nanny," he said.

"I assure you, I do not feel like your nanny."

She wish she hadn't have said that. Not quite the way she had. But then, maybe she just wished that he didn't make her feel… All of this.

He certainly didn't seem to have a problem eating what she had brought, cheeseburger or not, and she could feel him beginning to settle beside her.

And she just… Found that she enjoyed sitting next to him.

Especially as some of his tension began to resolve.

"I saw my mother," he said.

"What?"

"In the library. I caught you, and you looked so terrified… And it made me think of her. My mother. The way that she looked just as…"

"I'm sorry," she said.

"There is no need to be sorry. I was just explaining."

"But I am sorry. You've seen horrible things."

"The world can be horrible. This is a nice movie about a nice family. And Beth still dies."

It was such a pragmatic thing to say, and it almost made her laugh. Because he was right. Even being a good, normal family didn't protect you from tragedy.

Not that either of them would know. He'd had a good family, but they hadn't been normal, and it made them a target. And she'd had a very, very bad family.

"That's a grim outlook," she said.

"I don't think so," he said. "But then, it is entirely possible that my own viewpoint of the world is not… Entirely normal."

She had forgotten that there was kissing in this movie. It was incredibly mild. And yet… The tension between the characters, two people coming together at all, touching, felt fraught in the positions that she and Riyaz sat in.

He was half-naked.

And she…

She didn't have any experience with men. Her mind wandered. To the books that he'd read. But it also wandered to… The simple truth was he had been in a dungeon for sixteen years. She wondered if he'd had a lover before then.

She wondered…

Was it possible that he was actually…? Also a virgin?

The thought made her feel hot.

With her lack of experience, it made sense for her to moon after a man like Cairo. He would know exactly how to touch a woman.

And yet, as soon as she thought of that, she thought of the way it had felt to be held in Riyaz's strong arms.

She had never felt so… Protected. Even while she had been afraid, the way that he had encircled her in his strength had been…

What she knew was that he had protected her. Utterly and completely. Whatever threat he had seen… His intent had been to keep her safe.

The movie was ending, and there was another passionate kiss on-screen.

And in spite of herself, she looked between them. Their fingertips were close to touching, with the way they were seated on the blanket.

And then she looked up, her eyes meeting his.

She saw heat there, even in the darkness.

She looked away quickly.

He was bringing a woman here to marry. And he would need…

What he needed was to learn how to be around a woman. How to be softer.

She didn't need him to be soft with her. She didn't need him to be anything other than what he was.

She didn't know anything about the woman who would be coming to marry him.

But it would be different for her than it was for Brianna.

Brianna was trying to meet him where he was at and coach him. Help him.

Brianna had come from a background that was so far from normal that Riyaz didn't put her off at all.

Whatever woman married him… It was different. He needed to learn how to be *with* someone. He didn't even know how to compromise with the necessities of the world around him. Much less another person.

"I hope you enjoyed the movie," she said.

"Yes," he said.

"I'll leave you. But I hope that…"

"I don't want you to leave me," he said.

"Oh."

"I wish to go to the pool beneath the palace. Come with me."

"Why?" Her heart froze in her chest.

"Because I asked you to."

This was part of her job. Socializing with him.

Except she sort of wanted a break from him. She *needed* one.

She also wanted to be closer to him, and that was not her job.

Cairo was getting that woman right now.

And it was her job to prepare him for it. "Okay… I suppose I might need… A bathing suit?"

"Yes," he said. But there was something dark in his tone. And she wished that it didn't make her feel like he had touched her. But it did.

She let out a shuddering breath, and stood. "I'll clean all of this up…"

"Someone else will do it," he said. "I will meet you. At the top of the stairs."

"Okay. I'll meet you then."

He knew what he was doing. And he knew that it was unfair. But he also recognized that… She wanted him. The way that she had looked at him during the movie made it obvious. Even to him.

Because he could sense this thing between them. Like fire. Something electric.

He could feel it in the tightening of his body, and the answering look in her eyes.

He wanted her.

And he didn't see why he shouldn't have her.

He did not love Ariel. He was hardly saving himself for her.

He had not saved himself for anything. He had been… He had been manipulated. Controlled. And the first moment that he had seen the sun, he had seen Brianna, and it seemed a sign.

That she was his. And meant to be.

He wished to touch her. Taste her.

His brother had ensured that he was given a new wardrobe when he was set free. Along with that wardrobe had been a pair of black shorts that were supposed to be for swimming.

He put them on now, and went to the top of the dungeon stairs.

Several minutes later, Brianna appeared. She was wearing a fluffy pink robe over the top of whatever she had on beneath.

She attempted to look anywhere but his chest, and he was amused when her eyes couldn't quite stay away from his body.

Yes. He was right.

One thing he had learned was to be certain in all things. The dungeon had been his kingdom for many years. And everything within it in his control. How much he moved, how much he didn't. How much he slept. What he read, at least within the array of five books he had at any given time.

It made him very certain. Even outside of it.

And he did not need experience to know what the two of them wanted from each other.

Could they not just make each other feel good? That was all he wanted. It wasn't even about his own needs, though they were ferocious.

But about her desire.

How he longed to see her flush with it.

"Down this way," he said.

He still remembered. Of course he did. He hadn't thought much about his real life, not once he'd gone into the dungeon. He had read.

When he wasn't firmly in the present, he kept

his thoughts on fictional worlds. Fictional people. There he could read about love, desire, sex, anger, revenge, all while keeping distance between himself and those things. For they were contained in books, along with places he had not been, and foods he could not eat.

He had not wanted his entire world to be shrunk down to those stone walls.

He had not wanted them to be the only thing that he could see in front of him.

And reading had kept those pictures in his mind sharp.

Still, he had not thought about the walls immediately beyond the dungeon. The palace. His home. A home he was still in yet could not visit. So he had tried to erase it from his mind. Had done his best to simply…let it fade.

Yet he remembered it all now.

He remembered the underground pool area. All mosaic and pillars. A glimmering sort of underground cave of wonder. They had many happy times there as a family. A place where they could all relax and simply be themselves.

He was certain he would remember how to swim. That, he thought, had to be something buried into your muscle memory. It was a survival instinct, after all.

They walked down to the end of the corridor, down a spiral staircase and into the magnificent room, which was every bit as glorious as he remembered.

And he could remember laughing here. Playing here.

The memories were so sharp, but unlike that moment in the library, it did not intrude on reality. Didn't block out the moment.

"This is incredible," she said.

"Yes. It is."

He began to step down into the water. And then slid forward, slicing through like a knife.

And he found that he could swim. Expertly still.

"Come on," he said.

She looked at him, and he could see color mounted in her cheeks. Then she let the rope slide from her shoulders. Revealing a bright yellow bikini beneath.

And his body went hard like iron.

The body that she revealed surpassed his wildest dreams.

Her breasts were full, spilling from the yellow cups, her stomach soft, her waist small. Her hips were lush, and the way the bottom of the swimsuit caused her hips to dent inward, forced him to imagine what it would look like if he gripped them with his hands and held on tight.

She looked away from him, but she began to walk to the edge of the pool. "It is very nice-looking," she said, her voice suddenly stilted. Stiff.

"Well, it is much nicer than I even remembered. But I think perhaps my memories were blunted by design. Sometimes being able to remember good things felt like a gift. In other times it felt more like a curse."

She didn't say anything, but nodded, getting into the water, the surface lapping up over her hips. She shivered.

"You are lovely," he said.

Her skin went scarlet all over. "You shouldn't…"

"Should I pretend that I'm not looking at you? That I'm not taking careful inventory of each dip and swell of your body? Of the way your breasts look. Firm and glorious. Of your hips, how full and lush they are, and how I wish to grab hold of them."

"Riyaz…"

Her voice was breathless, but not a warning. He swam over to her. "Come," he said, extending his arm.

She hesitated for a moment, and then she reached out, taking his hand, and he pulled her toward him, swimming her out with him, her body pressed against his, and he groaned. "Brianna," he said. "You are… A temptation too many for me."

"Riyaz," she said. "This is not… We aren't…"

He reached up and moved his thumb over her lips. "What?"

"I can't help you with this. This isn't why I'm here. This isn't what Cairo wanted me to do."

"I see. Do you love my brother?"

"Yes," she said.

She looked away from him, clearly ashamed at the admission.

That was something he could not understand. The shame people felt around their feelings.

It was easy for him to talk about how beautiful she was. To admit that he wanted her. It felt absurd to deny such an obvious thing. He was hard, and he wanted to look his fill. He could hide neither of those things if she chose to see them.

And why should he be ashamed of them? She was a beautiful woman. And he was a man who had long been denied the sight and touch of a beautiful woman. Why would he not enjoy her?

And if she loved Cairo... He did not care for it. But he didn't see why she should be embarrassed. He gripped her chin and directed her face toward him. "Why?"

"He saved me," she said. "And has taken care of me ever since. And I'm in love with him. I... He is my friend. But..."

"Are you in love with him, or do you feel bound to him for what he did?"

"I love him," she said.

"And yet it doesn't prevent you from feeling attraction to me."

"I'm human. I said I loved your brother. I didn't say anything had ever happened between us."

"So you're saying you're hungry for the touch of the one you love, but as he has not put his hands on you... Your overall hunger for touch is greater than your need for him?" He moved his hands down her back, stopping just above the waistband of her bikini bottoms. How badly he wished to cup her luscious derrière. And yet he wished to wait. Until he had more explicit evidence of her desire.

"I just think… It is entirely possible to appreciate the looks of a person while loving another, isn't it? If it weren't, then people wouldn't have affairs."

"But this would not be an affair. You said yourself. My brother has never touched you."

"You are to be married."

"To a woman I don't love. To a woman I owe nothing to."

She wiggled in his hold, and he allowed her to extricate herself. He growled.

"Don't growl at me," she said.

"I wish to touch you," he said.

"We aren't touching. We're talking. I'm here to help you, and it isn't fair of me to take advantage of you."

He laughed, the sound echoing off the walls in the pool. "Take advantage of me? You are tiny. I could force you to do whatever I wished if I were that sort of man. You could not force me to do anything."

"Maybe not. But you have been in captivity for all these years. And how many women have you even been exposed to? Perhaps you only want me because of proximity. It would be taking advantage of you."

"That sounds like an excuse."

"It isn't. You're engaged. You've made that decision."

"Unless I imprison her."

"Her father betrayed you. Not her," she said, frowning.

He did not want her to frown.

"I know. But just as I am a symbol of hope to the people, whether I am fully within my right mind or not, Ariel will serve as recompense. Though, not in prison, but as my wife. Whether it was her sin or not. We cannot help what we symbolize. I am only sheikh because of who my father is. How is it any different that she is to be sheikha because of who her father is?"

She sank deeper into the water, swimming on her back. Away from him. "I know very well what it's like to suffer because of who your father is. To be used as a pawn. It isn't fair."

He swam to her, closing the distance between them, and wrapped his arm around her waist, pulling her to him. He groaned as her breasts made contact with his chest. She looked away, but he could see her pulse beating faster at the base of her throat. He lowered his head, and kissed her there.

The press of his mouth against that soft skin electrified him.

On impulse, he licked her neck, dragging his tongue slowly up, capturing the water droplets that lingered there.

She shook in his arms, a small cry escaping her lips.

"Riyaz," she said. "That's not… We can't."

"You like it."

"I'm talking about something serious," she said, pressing her hands against his chest and pushing herself away from him.

"Tell me," he commanded. "Your serious thing. Though I don't understand why I cannot hold you in my arms while you do."

"Because you *licked* me."

"Yes. You taste delicious."

"That isn't fair."

"I never said that I was fair."

"You're very frank," she said. "You're going to have to work on that. People don't just say whatever they think."

"And why not? It seems to me that it is the duplicity in the world that creates problems. Not honesty. Not frankness. I don't understand why these different things are issues. Why should you not love Cairo and also want me? Why should you be ashamed of either of those things? Why should I hide the fact that I find you beautiful? None of it makes sense to me. It is duplicity that killed my family. Honesty harms no one. You loving Cairo... It harms no one. Who does not wish to be loved? He should be pleased."

"It is embarrassing," she said. "Because when you love someone, and they do not return the feeling, it is painful. Because you feel foolish and exposed to want someone when they had never demonstrated that they want you."

"He would have to be an idiot not to want you."

"I should say... With Cairo... I'm not sure that

him *wanting* me would feel especially flattering. He is not discriminate when it comes to sexual partners. It's a hobby to him. Some people run every morning when they wake up. I think your brother takes a new lover. He's not particular."

He chuckled. "How nice for him. When I tell you that I think you're beautiful, I mean I have never looked at another woman and had the same feelings. Or the same thoughts."

"You also haven't seen very many women. I'm just guessing."

"No. But then, it sounds to me as if you're just choosing not to be flattered. Because it is easier."

"How is it easier?"

"You're afraid of what would happen if you believed me. That you were beautiful."

She looked away from him. "Being beautiful has never given me anything. My father…" She looked back up at him. "None of this is about me. None of this is about my life. We are supposed to be talking about you. It's you that I'm supposed to be concerned about."

"How long has it been since anyone concerned themselves with you? Who came alongside you? Cairo rescued you, but did he do this for you? Did he speak to you? Did he try to teach you how to live in the world? Eat the same breakfast as you, and watch movies with you?"

She looked away. "No. He didn't. But I was fifteen, and he was nineteen. And we would not have…

It's simply not how that relationship would've worked. He sent me to school. He was establishing his business, his fortune. He didn't need a girl hanging on to him and…"

"Perhaps you should let me listen to you. Perhaps it would be a good thing."

"My father wanted to sell me. What do you think of that? To pay his debts. I was pretty enough. His rival wanted to buy me, and then sell me continually. To whatever men might want to pay for an evening. Or few moments. That is what being pretty meant when I was fifteen. And maybe part of why I love Cairo so much as he didn't treat me like being pretty was all I was. And he certainly didn't use it as an excuse to touch me or ask for payment for what he did for me. Maybe that is why I cared for him so much."

Fury rushed through him. Fury. That any man could think to put their hands on her when she did not wish them to. That her own father would treat her so.

He had tasted betrayal. A man his father trusted had ultimately led to his death. Had led to Riyaz's imprisonment. But his own father had fought to the death to save him. To save his wife, to save his sons.

He had never known the betrayal of family.

His family had loved them.

"Does your father still live?"

"As far as I know," she said.

"He will not for long. I will find him. And I will have him killed."

"You can't just…do that," she said.

"Yes, I can. I command entire armies. I can certainly command a small group of assassins to take out the human garbage that would dare do such a thing to you."

"This isn't *listening*, Riyaz."

"I have heard everything that I need to. The world would be better off if he was not wasting its oxygen."

It was the strangest thing, he could tell that he frightened her, and yet he could also see a small amount of pleasure reflected in her eyes. She was glad that he wished to protect her.

"I will always protect you," he said. "Brianna, you never have need to fear for your safety."

"Riyaz, that is very kind of you. It is… I'm not your responsibility. You're mine. You're a job that I have to do. Your brother has asked me to and… You and I have known each other for two days."

Was that all? Time had so little meaning to him. And he had very much not met many people in these past years, so there was something about this time that he had spent with her that felt deep. That felt timeless.

This moment in the baths could've been weeks.

This revelation of looking at her, of having a few stolen moments of holding her in his arms.

Though he would not grab hold of her. Not again. Not after what she had said about her father. Not after hearing that her father had wanted to sell her.

She would need to come to him. She would need

to be the one to draw her body against his, and then he would hold her, move his hands over her.

He wished to do that.

To touch her everywhere. To kiss her.

He had to be certain it was what she wanted.

He was certain of many things. Not the least of which being that she was attracted to him.

But the reality of what she had been through… He didn't know what else her father might have subjected her to.

He did not know enough about her. And he was hungry for more, and yet she did not seem to wish to share. She seemed to only want to throw her trauma out as a weapon.

"I will protect you," he said. "I pledge myself to you."

"How can you do that?"

"Life has been simple for me, these past sixteen years. It is a funny thing. Because while I might resent that Cairo had access to certain things. Certain freedoms. He also had to do all this work. And he lived a life of complexity. Apparently that has included an endless string of lovers, which, I will not deny I am slightly envious of. I had to *survive* every day. And that is all. I had to care for my body. The day that lay before me from the time I woke to the time I slept was incredibly simple. There was very little in the way of decision-making to be done. I was in control, for all that I was not in charge of whether or not I left the dungeon. That has actually made me incredibly certain in moments like these.

"You think that I've not known you long enough, and yet to me, this is the deepest I have known someone in sixteen years. Deeper even than Cairo, who has not been around. I have shared things with you that I have not shared with anyone else, and now you have shared things with me. It is the simplest thing in the world to pledge you my allegiance. That I promise you."

"Riyaz…" She looked away for a moment, then took a breath and met his gaze. "I appreciate that. But this is a job for me. Nothing more. And when it's over I'm going to go back to my life. I'm going to have a normal life. Someday. This has been somewhat clarifying for me. I am too attached to Cairo, and that needs to stop. I can't afford it. This… This attachment. I need to make my own life. And this is the beginning of me stepping away from him. My feelings for him. All of that. I want to find a normal man, and I want to have a normal family. I want to live in a normal neighborhood. Not some town house that there's no way I could ever afford. I've never had normal. I've never even seen it outside of a book. But can you imagine that? A little house in a neighborhood. Where kids can ride their bikes. My kids. That's what I want. That's what I want more than anything. Normal."

"I see," he said. "I know the normal that you're talking about. I've read about it. But we talked about this earlier, and the truth remains. Normal will never protect you. I will."

"Thank you. I will keep that in mind."

He felt her withdraw before she physically began to do so.

"Were you hurt?"

She was halfway out of the water and stopped. "I'm sorry, what?"

"Had your father sold you before?"

A crease appeared between her brows. "Are you asking if I was assaulted?"

"Yes. Either way, I owe you an apology. I held you because I thought you were beautiful. And I wanted to touch you. I assumed that you wanted the same thing, but I did not make sure. And now that you've told me these things…"

"I wasn't," she said. "But I appreciate you asking. I… I did want you to hold me. It's only that I thought better of it."

"I can't understand that either." The empty cavern of misunderstanding in him seemed endless.

"What? Thinking better of something?"

"I was denied a great many things being locked away. I don't understand why you would deny yourself, with all the freedom that you have."

"Says the man who is opting to eat the same porridge every day? Sometimes you deny yourself because you know that something is too much for you to handle, Riyaz. That's why. Can you not understand that? Can you not see that I have to…? I have to protect myself."

"Then you had best go. I wish to protect you from me. But if you stay… I will find it harder and harder to do so, particularly now that I have confirmed that you enjoyed being held."

She finished getting out of the pool, and went to collect her robe. She hesitated for a moment, and then pulled it on. Then she looked back at him one more time before walking away.

She had no idea what had just happened. Her body and all the rest of her was still buzzing the next day at breakfast.

Riyaz didn't come to breakfast, and she didn't go looking for him. He was probably in the dungeon. Instead, she sat there over a plate of waffles—they had stocked the palace with American foods for her, one of Cairo's thoughtful gestures, damn him for being so good—reflecting on what it had felt like to be held against Riyaz's strong body. On why she had shared anything about her past with him and why… Why she had admitted that she liked him touching her.

Maybe because she couldn't stand him feeling guilty.

He was so blunt and strange, and he asked all kinds of things that he shouldn't. That polite, normal people would know not to ask. But he was neither polite nor normal. So he had just gone and asked after her potential trauma as if it was as easy as yes or no.

But then he made it very clear why. He hadn't wanted to be part of taking away her choice. And she couldn't help but marvel at the sensitivity, for all that the man didn't seem to have an excess of it.

And she had felt like she couldn't lie to him. Of course she had enjoyed him touching her. The press of his lips against her neck... It had kept her awake.

She wondered why he had kissed her there. She wondered why any of it. Why had she told him that she loved Cairo? And why had she confessed her deepest dreams... Being normal. Living in a regular house.

She was supposed to be taking care of him. She was supposed to be helping him. And yet she had ended up... Talking to him as if he was her therapist or something and... It was all just wrong.

She had never gotten attached to somebody that she was working with like this.

And they had only known each other for two days. The way that he had dismissed that, as if it was so obvious that the two days they had spent together were more significant than the time suggested.

And it was. She couldn't explain why. She only knew that it was.

When she was halfway through her waffles, he strode into the room. "My brother has collected Ariel."

"Oh," she said, her heart slamming against her breastbone. "She is not amenable to the marriage.

Which is unfortunate. But he said he cannot bring her here now."

"Right. Well…" She knew that was because of her. Because of the report that she had given back to Cairo, but she hesitated to admit it to Riyaz.

She needed him to be able to focus and not have distractions, that much was true. So maybe she could express that without admitting that she had actually told Cairo that she feared slightly for Ariel's safety. She wasn't sure that was true anymore. She didn't think Riyaz was dangerous. Not in that way.

"What is this?" he said, gesturing to the plate that was in his spot.

"Belgian waffles. I thought you would probably like them."

"Are you going to lecture me on self-denial?"

"I was thinking about it. Since you had so much to say about mine."

"All right. I will try the waffles."

"Why don't you try having three adventurous meals with me today."

"All right. Will you let me hold you again?"

"To what end?"

"I don't understand. *To what end*. Did you not enjoy being held?"

"Yes. But men don't typically wish to *hold* women unless there is an end point."

"By which you mean sex."

"Yes," she said, heat rushing through her body. "By which I mean sex."

"I would not be opposed to sex."

"No. I can't."

"Then you will have to come to me when you decide to change your mind."

That simple. And yet, she felt like her body was burning. Boiling with need and anticipation. And somehow she felt… Disappointed at his proclamation that he wouldn't push her. Part of her, she found, wished that he would.

"Why do you think I'll change my mind?" she asked.

"I may not have a lot of practical experience in the world. But I have read what the greatest minds have to say about love. About attraction. About rage and revenge. Desire. Heartbreak. I have read enough to know that there is a certain amount of inevitability to desire. In part because I think when people desire someone, they will come up with whatever excuses possible to give in to that desire. We resist because…"

"Why do we resist?" she asked.

Her heart was thundering so hard she was sure that he would be able to hear it. She knew that she was being provocative and asking him. Implying that what he thought, what he *wanted*, was not valid because he had never lived out among people.

It was mean.

"I have read about these things," he said, his confidence absolute. "I think people resist because they are afraid. There are many foolish reasons to be afraid. Afraid of what other people think. I'm not certain that I could ever find it in me to care about what someone thinks. Afraid of their own responses, that I can understand. Not for myself personally. Only some people have experiences that make them afraid. That they would grow too attached to the partner."

"I see. And which do you think I am?"

The way that he smiled, slow and seductive, made her stomach clench tight. "I'm afraid that you would fall in love with me."

She couldn't help it. She laughed. "You're afraid that I would fall in love with you? That is quite the ego you have."

"Let me rephrase. I think you are *afraid* that you might fall in love with me. That is what holds you back. Because otherwise, what do you care? Cairo never has to know. No one ever has to know."

"I can't live like that. I could not keep something like that from a man that I consider to be one of my closest friends."

"You are required to divulge intimate details from your life to him? I find that very strange."

"Well, it isn't up to you to find it strange or not. I didn't ask."

"Does he let you know every time he takes a lover?"

"I don't have that kind of time."

"Yes, so frequent is the act for my brother," he said, the disdain in his voice almost amusing.

"I don't want to talk about this," she said. "I'm here to help you."

"You can imagine why I might not find that appealing. I feel that I have a connection with you, *habibti*." He had never called her that before. She knew that it was an endearment, but she wasn't sure quite what it meant. "I have not met many people. Cairo might be your friend, but you are the closest that I have to such a thing. Do you not see why it might be... Problematic, for you to act as if you are here to serve me, and nothing more?"

She was angry. Because she *liked* him. Because he wasn't just a job. She had sat and talked to him, she had been held in his arms, and she felt connection to him.

She just didn't *want* to. Couldn't afford to.

"It isn't like that. It isn't that I don't... Find you interesting. But this is a job I'm supposed to do before I go back to my life. And *this* is your life. I'm going to leave it."

"So what would be the problem in indulging your desire?"

Again, the words were so seductive. So...

"Because, Riyaz, that isn't how I'm wired. I don't just have flings with men. If I did... Well, I had plenty of opportunity. But for me, desire can't be separated from feelings."

He looked smug. "So you *are* afraid, then, that you will fall in love with me."

"I am not afraid of any such thing."

No, what scared her the most was the way that she felt so drawn to him. So attracted, in spite of it being Cairo who theoretically held her heart.

She had to let go of Cairo. She truly did. When she had talked to him last night to give him an update, all she had been able to tell him was that he needed to keep Ariel away.

She hadn't seen the other woman. She wondered how beautiful she was.

Why did it matter if she was beautiful? Riyaz had nothing to do with her.

Maybe she was just jealous because Cairo was off with another woman. Except that was basically a day ending in Y.

Cairo had any number of partners at any given time. None of them seemed to affect him emotionally. And because it didn't affect him she wasn't all that jealous, not really. Anyway, she had somewhat accepted that he would always be out of her reach. That she would always be pining, with absolutely no chance of ever being anything else.

But her feelings for him were still there. Though maybe they were just a shield. Something safe. Something that kept her separate from other people. From other men.

And her attraction to Riyaz… It just kept on growing. And the way that he wanted to talk about it, the way that he just openly acknowledged it…

"Do you know, I have been in love with your brother for sixteen years. And at no point have we ever discussed those feelings. Or my attraction to him. That just isn't something people do. Because it *is* embarrassing, whether you understand it or not. You're supposed to leave those kinds of things unspoken. Because they're intimate. And out of respect for the other person's feelings…"

"Why do you leave these things unspoken? So that you can sit and long with no hope of ever having your feelings returned? So that you can wonder? Is that it? Is it to live in a space of magic, where you can convince yourself that perhaps it could be real? Do you wish to have a story that you tell yourself? Is that it? And if you were to confess your feelings to him, he might say *no*. And then your hope would die. You would have no more stories left to tell yourself."

It was such an unflattering, bracing truth. And she didn't like it. She also had to acknowledge that it was probably true.

"It's the truth. For all of humanity," she bit out.

"I had no choice but to live lives that were not mine," he said. "I had no choice but to live lives that were stories. I have read about how incendiary the touch between two lovers can be. And if I'd had my choice, I would have made that touch real. Reading is magic, but it is not life. You have had all these opportunities, but you haven't taken them. I can understand in some small part why you might wish to protect yourself from the truth, but the reality is, it does nothing for you. It does nothing for anyone. You might live, and let you save all that you desire for imagination. No. That I cannot understand."

"You are about to take over the throne. To rule this country. And you're worried about my... Honesty."

"That I will rule Nazul is a fact. A reality of the birth order in my family, and my lineage. It is not an achievement. And yes, I must work to be... To be seen as fit to do these things. I understand that. But it does not inspire my passion. It does not intrigue me. My life has been about small details, and the small details have... Expanded. The possibilities."

"Eat your waffles. Consider those an infinite sensual possibility."

"I'm not certain that waffles can be called sensual."

"Well, that's because you didn't eat them fresh. Believe me when I tell you, they are probably better than sex."

She shouldn't have said that. And she realized that when she felt the sharp, keen stare coming from him.

"And would you know that for certain?"

"What exactly are you asking me?"

"I think you know. Would you know for certain if the waffles were better than sex?"

"I have a very rich fantasy life," she said.

"So you are a virgin."

"I don't think of myself that way. I'm not defined by whether or not a man has touched me."

"I did not suggest that you were."

And it burned. Her desire to ask him if he was the same. She was too embarrassed. Tongue-tied.

"The waffles are fine," he said. And then he strode over to where she sat at the end of the table, took her hand in his and lifted her into a standing position. "Do you know what I need help with?"

Her heart was thundering radically, and for a moment, she thought he was going to do something like… Press her hand to the front of his pants and allow her to feel his hardness there. The evidence of his desire. Or perhaps he would lower his head and kiss her.

"Teach me to dance."

CHAPTER SIX

THE CONVERSATION AT breakfast had him aching. He wanted an excuse to touch her again. To hold her.

She was such a strange woman. Or maybe she wasn't. He didn't have much experience of women. Or of any human. Maybe all people were like this. Denying what they wanted so that they could live in fantasy land.

He did not see the point of it. It was so... They were all prisoners. People.

Prisoners to all of these made-up prisons.

You still sleep in the dungeon.

Yes. He did. It was called the transition. There was hardly a handbook on how to escape the dungeon. If there were, he would've read it. Though, if it existed, his captors never would've brought it to him, so maybe that was untrue. But either way, he felt that he was handling it as well as anyone could. And even then, what did it matter? What did any of it matter?

There was no grade being given out.

And yet, she was so careful. Brianna.

Sunshine and raspberries and Brianna.

He half expected her to deny the request. But instead, she squared her shoulders and looked at him, her expression defiant. "Of course. Is there a room where you would prefer to conduct the lessons?"

"The library. I imagine it is cleaned up."

"Yes. The staff saw to that quickly. They thought that it might be upsetting to you to see the aftermath."

"It's not upsetting to me."

"Maybe there is something to the way that you spent the last sixteen years, because you don't seem particularly concerned or guilty about anything. You don't seem to harbor a whole lot of bad feelings." She looked away. "I'm sorry. Of course that isn't true. The issue that you had yesterday, it obviously speaks to some deeper things…"

"I don't need you to validate me. I'm fine. And you are correct. Living the way that I did, I could not afford to indulge these sorts of concerns. Why would they matter? These are abstract things. The thing that frustrated me the most about being in captivity was what I could not do for others. For my country. I had to accept the fact that my existence needed to be all about my survival. That is different than enjoying life or living for others, serving others. But when you have no other people to worry about, when the only people who you are in view of are your enemies, your captives, then what opinions have you to be concerned about? Also guilt… I have no guilt or shame. That is also connected to the expectations of others."

"Well, you are a singular person. Because most of us worry an awful lot about what other people think."

"Who do you worry about?" He extended his hand, giving her time to decide if she was going to take it. She did, and he led her toward the library. The touch of her hand to his was a spark. And he reveled in it. It was entirely possible that this was the only contact he would ever have with her. Their palms touching. Her body pressed against his in the pool. Her pulse beneath his lips.

That might be all there was. It was more than he'd ever had.

And yet, the idea of not claiming her fully felt wrong. The beast within him roared, but he did not growl out loud. Which was for her. Only for her. Because he didn't care whether he did or not.

They opened the doors to the library, and closed them behind them.

"I can play some music on my phone. Maybe there's something traditional…"

"Yes. Because there is a wedding dance, you know, and I will have to be in practice for that."

She did not look pleased about that. And he found that it ignited a spark of pleasure in his gut.

"I will have to hold you in my arms."

"That's okay," she said, the words hushed.

He went forward and took her in his arms, held her against his body as they began to move in time to the music. And it was the strangest thing, because he didn't remember. As if he was in another place, another time. But not in that dark way he had gone to it yesterday. It was something different. And so was he.

As if the weight of the past wasn't pressing down on him. As if perhaps he was different. And maybe she was too.

"Brianna Whitman," he said. "Your father was a bad man. Was all of your childhood bad?"

She shook her head. "No. Because I didn't know that we weren't normal. I didn't know... I didn't realize my father wasn't like other fathers. I thought that I was happy enough. I really did. I thought that perhaps... I thought that perhaps we were maybe only a little bit different to other families. We had a very big house. And it was behind a large gate. My father was rarely around. My mother... My mother left when I was about eleven. But I'll never know if that's actually what happened. Because that's when it began to become clear to me that my father wasn't a good man. My father in fact is a very bad man. I don't know if he hurt my mother. I don't know if she ran away and had to hide, couldn't take us because of the danger that it would represent. And I may never know. Cairo has tried to locate her before, but he's never been able to. Whatever happens, I'm not angry with her. I know that my father would never have shown her mercy. If she had taken us... He would've chased her down for the rest of her life. Because we were nothing but collateral for him. Property. My oldest sister, he married her off to his right-hand man. And that just left me. But it wasn't marriage that he wanted for me. It was something else. To appease a rival. And that is when I really knew. That's when I really knew he didn't love me. He never had. It was broken, and it could never be anything else."

"What did you do to find joy in those times? Because we all find joy. I grew up a spoiled prince. The heir to the throne. Very little was ever denied me. The one bit of freedom that I knew I would never have is the ability to choose my own bride. But… My behavior, my actions were never going to be hindered by that. I knew it. So they had chosen this pretty American girl for me, but if I did not wish to bed her every night for the rest of my life I didn't have to. I could take mistresses. Other wives. It was not popular in modern society, but it didn't mean I couldn't. *Nothing* was off-limits to me. At sixteen, the world stretched before me, mine entirely. One thing I could have never imagined was what it would be like to lose that. And yet I did. In a moment." He released hold on her for a moment and snapped his finger. "In a moment, I lost it. Do you know what that's like? That change. So abrupt. But I was not miserable for the entirety of those sixteen years. If I had been, I would have surely descended into madness. Part of what we do is find ways to survive. In ways to make that survival bearable. What did you do to make your survival bearable?"

He found that he wanted to know. Desperately.

More than anything, in fact. She was the most fascinating creature he had ever seen. Ever known. And maybe the list of creatures he had seen and known was short, but it did not matter. It was still true.

"Like you, I enjoyed reading. I also loved movies. Movies about families. Who sat around the dinner table every night. And I loved sitcoms. Where there was always a lesson, and everyone was safe. At home every night, in a house with parents who loved them. I loved it, because it gave me hope that those things existed."

"As you said, you want normal."

"Yes. I want what I saw then. I want that thing I saw in all of those homes. I crave it. And I've never been able to have it. Maybe some of that's my fault. My situation with Cairo is hardly normal. And that is of my own making."

She looked down, and a lock of silky red hair fell into her face. He reached up and touched it, pushing it back off of her forehead. She looked up at him.

"Maybe the thing is you are not normal. And that is not a bad thing. I think that you are singular, Brianna. Why should you contort yourself to fit this ideal?"

She looked desolate. "I want to be happy. I really want to be happy."

"Not in the way that we have made ourselves happy in the past."

She shook her head. "No. Not in that way. Not in that way where we have to take just moments of joy and hope for the best. Hope that someday we get to feel it again."

"What do you feel now?"

Her face went red. "Tell me. Because you do not have to pretend with me. I despise pretense, as you are now well aware. Tell me what you feel. You do not need to make stories for me."

"You are very warm," she said. "And a surprisingly good dancer."

"It shocked me that I remembered. But like swimming, I guess it does not go away."

"You make me… You make my heart beat faster." She couldn't look at him, he noticed. "You make my body feel like it's too sensitive."

"Too sensitive for what?" Desire gathered at the base of his spine, tightened within him. "Or is it something that I could help with?"

Then she did something unexpected. She reached up and touched his face, her fingertips dragging down his cheek, along his jawbone. "I keep thinking about those moments of joy. Taking moments, even though you know they won't sustain you forever. Even though you know they can't last. I… Maybe there's something to that."

Without thought, he turned his head and pressed his mouth to her palm.

He was hard now. His desire a raging beast, and he knew that if he actually did take her to bed he would have to find a way to take it slow. He would have to put her pleasure first.

And he would give thanks for all the times that he read books that left him hard and unsatisfied in the end, because they were lessons. Because they had taught him about female pleasure, and the way that it had to be treated. Because he had learned that a woman could reach her peak over and over again, even if a man could only reach it once in a prescribed amount of time. He had learned all the ways to make a woman wet. To make her desperate.

That was what he wanted if he was going to take Brianna as a lover.

It was not about his own needs, not simply. For his needs were linked with hers.

He wanted her to desire him.

He *needed* her to.

Her eyelids fluttered closed, and a small, tortured sound escaped her lips.

"Do you want me?"

"What would either of us know about it?" she whispered.

He chuckled. Finally, she was saying what was on her mind rather than holding back.

"I know that what I wish is to kiss you until you are begging for more. I know that I should take it slowly, teasing your nipples over your clothes, putting my hand between your thighs and stroking. Touch you until you are arching against me, until you are asking for more. And only then should I give it to you. Or maybe not. Maybe I should keep it back. Keep more to myself, until you are willing to *beg*. Then, and only then, will I begin to kiss you down your neck, reveal your body slowly to my gaze, expose your breasts. So that I can taste them. I crave that. Your skin. The sensation of sucking your nipples deep into my mouth. And then, I would kiss my way down your body. You have the most beautiful body. The sight of you in that bikini nearly sent me to hell. Or heaven. I'm not certain which it is. I would kiss my way down your soft stomach. Part your legs. And I have no shame, as you know. So I would look my fill until you turned bright red. Until you were begging for me to either let you close your legs and walk away, or feast upon you. And then… I would not. I wouldn't do either, because when I take you, Brianna, you will surrender your control to me. You will trust that I will listen to the cues of your body and give you the pleasure that you want. That you need. You have had any number of years to find the keys to your own desire. But when I have you like that, willing, beneath me, you will surrender to my will. I will kiss your thigh. I will not touch my tongue to that bundle of nerves that's crying out for my attention. I will make you quiver. Press a kiss low to your stomach, until you are begging me, and only then will I please us both by allowing myself a taste of your honey."

"Riyaz," she said, her voice trembling.

"Do you not wish to hear more?"

"It's a little bit like reading ahead in a book, isn't it?" she whispered.

Yes. She was seduced. He was certain of that. She had not said no.

She was choosing this. Him. She was choosing him.

And the need between them. The short moment of joy that they might find in one another's arms.

"No spoilers?" he asked.

"Where did you even hear that?"

"I read it."

She shook her head. "You are astonishing."

"Thank you. But I haven't even touched you yet."

"Riyaz… Kiss me. Please."

And he did not need to be asked twice.

He lowered his head, and Brianna bracketed his face with her palms. Felt the roughness of his whiskers against her skin.

And she wanted to weep.

And then his mouth was on hers, over hers. And it was… It was all that she could have ever fantasized about and more.

She didn't know what would happen after this. He was marrying another woman. And even if he weren't, he was the heir to the throne of this desert kingdom, and that had nothing to do with that sitcom family life that she wanted.

And they were… They could never be together. Not really. His reference point for everything was books. Hers TV. They were pretend people, playing the part of being real. But not with each other.

They had found honesty, *real* honesty here. And

she wanted it. More than anything. And maybe this was the gift. Just the moment. And whatever happened after didn't actually matter.

Maybe the gift was these few days, weeks, however long it was, of honesty.

He was the first person that she really felt like might understand her. And she had never thought she needed that. But she had put on a mask and a veneer from the moment that she had left her father's compound, and she had operated in the world with that mask. She had taught other people to do the same. She was teaching him to do it now, and for the first time, she felt some misgivings about that.

Maybe the problem with sitcoms was they were all on a set. Was that they were inherently *not* real.

And neither was she.

Except right now, she felt real. His lips parted, and his tongue swept deep into her mouth. She was shocked by the precision and skill present in that kiss. The way that he called need up from within her body without even trying.

He was a quick study, was Riyaz. And apparently, very good at getting information just by reading.

He reached around, his hand cupping the back of her head, as he kissed her deeper. His other arm was wrapped tightly around her body, holding her to him, and she wrapped her arms around his neck, her breasts pressed flat against his hard chest. Her heart was raging. Her whole body felt like it was on fire.

And everything up until this moment had only ever been a pale promise of this sort of passion.

For her, desire was so rooted in the unimaginable. In the thwarted desire that she felt for Cairo. But that was all hazy, and he was right. Riyaz was right. It was just a story. And the story was never anything more than images that you painted in your own mind. Or set pieces for a show.

But it wasn't substantial.

It wasn't real.

This was real. It was hard and sharp. There was nothing gauzy or easy about it. It was the rage of her own heartbeat, the warmth of his mouth, the slick friction of his tongue. The hard hold of his hand in her hair, the steel band of his arm.

It was need and fire. Temptation.

And when he swept her up off the floor, holding her in his arms like a warrior with a conquest, she knew that he didn't care who saw.

And it made her not care either.

This was their moment. Their pleasure. Their freedom.

He opened the doors to the library, and walked down the corridor. There was no ceremony, no concern that there were other people wandering around the palace. He did not pause for any questioning gazes, nor did he offer any explanations.

And she loved it. She truly did love it.

Maybe, maybe later, there would be cause for regret. Maybe she would be sorry that she did this. But she would've made a mistake. One that was her own.

That was normal. Trying things. Seizing the moment. The good feelings. The desire.

She could have this. Why not? Why not take what she wanted?

She had been frozen all this time. Wanting a man she couldn't have.

She wanted Riyaz, so who cared what came in the future? It was her choice. And there was something powerful in that.

He opened the door to his bedchamber, which she had personally never seen him anywhere near, and brought her inside, closing the door behind them and turning the lock.

Her heart thundered erratically as he stepped away from her, and removed his shirt.

She had seen him half-naked before, but this was different. Because he was looking at her with intent, and she knew that it wasn't going to simply be a look. She knew that it would be more. His hands on her body. Her hands on his.

She knew that it would be everything.

And it felt right. To give this to him. To be part of what he was giving himself. Because who else would ever understand? Who else would ever know?

Who else?

He moved forward, reached behind her and took hold of the zipper of her dress, and dragged it down,

the fabric falling away from her body, and uncere-
moniously dropping to the floor.

She hadn't given a lot of thought to the underwear
that she had on today, and now she wished she had.
Since she was standing before him in nothing more
than plain, serviceable white underwear.

But he did not seem to mind. Not at all. His gaze
was hungry as it roamed over her curves, and she had
never felt more beautiful than she did in that moment.

He moved toward her, taking her in his arms
again, and kissing her. "I have a promise to keep," he
whispered against her skin. And then he turned his
attention back to her mouth. Kissing her and kissing
her until she was dizzy with it. With her own need.
With the desperation of her desire for him. Until she
was trembling, until she was ready to beg, just as he
had promised her she would be.

His touch was almost unbearable, she was so hy-
persensitive. She wanted his hands directly on her
bare skin, but she also didn't know if she could endure it.

But then his eyes locked with hers, dark and hungry, and she knew that whatever was ahead... She
wanted it. She wanted this. She wanted him.

And somewhere in there, she felt powerful. That
this was a choice she was making—good or bad—
like a very normal girl.

Except how many normal girls got to experience sex for the first time with a man who looked
like him?

He was incredible. There was something raw about him. Something feral. It was always a strange thing when he opened his mouth and began to talk about books. He didn't have the look of a cerebral man.

And then he growled, that growl that he did, and she was reminded. That while he might possess the ability to reason, to be rational. That while he might discuss books and philosophize about why people behaved the way they did...

There was an elemental quality to him. And when he receded to that place—as he had done in the library that day when he had nearly killed a man with his bare hands—he was all in it. Just as he was now.

Right now, she had the beast.

And somehow, she felt safe even still.

He stroked her cheek, then tore her bra away from her body, the movement abrupt and unexpected.

And she gasped. Not because it was unpleasant. Not at all. It was what she wanted. He was what she wanted. And there she was, naked before him, and she reveled in it. Gloried in it. In this moment of ecstasy. Of raw, unbridled feeling.

The truth of it was, people like them... They had to learn to hide their feelings. It was a matter of survival.

She knew that, and she imagined that he did too.

"Give me all of it," she whispered, not meaning to speak, but not being able to control it either.

"All of what?"

"Your fury. Your feelings. Everything that you've always kept back. Because you had to, didn't you? To survive. Even if it wasn't out of fear of your captor, you couldn't allow yourself to go to dark places, or how would you live?"

He looked at her body, his expression on fire. "Do you want to talk?"

"No. I don't. I want to feel. Everything that I never let myself feel. But I want you to come with me. I don't want you to go easy on me. I don't want you to be gentle. I don't want you to treat me like I might break."

"You may regret saying that."

"But I said it. So now you know. It's my choice."

"Good."

He grabbed her waist, lifted her up off the ground, and licked one breast, then another. She shuddered, and he carried her over to the bed, holding her as if she was insubstantial. As if she weighed nothing.

And then he laid her out on the large, sumptuously appointed bed, his eyes roaming over her curves hungrily.

"And now," he said. "I can see the point and purpose to a bed."

He pressed his knee into the mattress, moved up to her body and cupped her breast with his hand. He watched, with rapt attention as he slid his thumb over her nipple. She felt it pucker. An arrow of pleasure hitting sharp and true between her legs.

"Riyaz," she said.

"Is it good?"

"Yes," she said. "It's good. Please. More. Please."

"It is amazing," he said. "You would not even tell my brother that you desired him, but you will beg me for my touch. Openly. Always be so honest with me," he said. "There is no room for embarrassment or shame. Not with us."

She shook her head, biting her lip as he pinched her nipple. As he moved his hand to her other breast and transferred his attentions there.

He moved his hands down her body, the strong, calloused fingers making her shiver as they trailed over her skin.

He hooked his thumbs into the sides of her panties and dragged them down her legs. And she didn't feel shame. As if his words had been an incantation. A magic spell. As if he had caused it to be so simply with his intonations.

He was magic. Or maybe they were.

"I thought of this, for all those years. Sixteen years, I thought of a woman's body. Various pieces of my imagination put together with images I had seen. Something to make an erotic slideshow in my head. But it was nothing. Nothing compared to you. Compared to the reality of your beauty. You are every promise fulfilled, Brianna. You are all that I desire. And how I desire you." He leaned forward, sucked her nipple deep into his mouth, the growl that rose in his throat gratifying her. She was becoming so fond of that growl.

Her back arched up off the mattress, and he sucked her deep until she was crying out his name.

Then he kissed his way down her stomach. And he did exactly as he promised. He pressed his lips to her inner thigh, beat a path to where she was slick with her need for him.

But that was when he lost his restraint. He reached around and took a handful of her rear, lifting her up off the bed and bringing her to his mouth as he began to feast upon her as if she was all that he had been denied. As if she was everything that he could ever want.

He lapped at her, concentrating on that sensitized bundle of nerves there, finding it unerringly. She gripped his hair, forked her fingers through it. Held him there. He moved his head, penetrating her with his tongue before sliding back up to where she was greedy for him. Could she even tell where she was greedy for him? She was greedy all over. She was desperate for him. For all that they could find together.

She was an expert at trying to find pure joy in moments. And this moment was perfect. She didn't want to see the end of it. She didn't want to see anything but this room. But them. His glorious, bronze skin, the play of his muscles. The intensity of his need for her as he pleasured her.

Desire tightened low in her stomach. Twisting, deeper, deeper. He licked her, then penetrated her with two fingers, and she cursed, shouting out his name and an obscenity all at once.

He growled again.

And again. He worked his fingers in and out of her body, his tongue relentless, and finally she shattered. Need pouring over her like a relentless storm. Then he moved away from her, his eyes never leaving her body as he moved his hands to the closure of his pants and solemnly divested himself of them. Leaving his body exposed to her.

He was thick and proud and she was shocked by how utterly glorious she found him.

There was a woman that she had coached once, trying to help her with some situations at work. She had told her that penises were fine, but she wouldn't be hanging up any art of them in her home.

She thought that she might actually want art of Riyaz in all his glory. Yes, she thought she might want that quite a lot.

She rose up on her knees and pressed her palms to his chest, watched as they slid down over his muscles, rippled over the glorious definition there. "You're beautiful," she said. "How dare they? How dare they hide you away."

He grabbed her wrist, lifted her palm to his mouth and kissed it. Then her wrist, the inside of her elbow, and she shivered. "Riyaz," she whispered.

"Brianna. I do like saying your name."

"I love to hear you say it."

She reached out and wrapped her hand around

his arousal, as if she had all the confidence of a woman who had done this before, when she very much did not.

But he felt good in her hand, and his expression was like ecstasy when he let his head fall back as she stroked him.

And then, it was like something jolted in him, a bolt of electricity, and he opened his eyes, watching her as she stroked him.

"I don't want to miss it," he said. "Because you look so beautiful like that."

And she had the thought that she knew how she might look even more beautiful to him. And again, she led with intuition rather than experience. She flicked her tongue over the head of his arousal, and then took part of him in. His growl was a whole force, as he canted his hips forward and drove himself deeper.

She took him in as deep as she could, but he was so large. She used her hand to help as she bobbed her head up and down, glorying in the taste of him. In the way she made him shake.

He was a man who had survived the unimaginable. And she made him tremble.

There was something glorious in that.

Who needed normal when she had this? Who needed normal, when there was all this power?

She pleasured him like that until she could feel the edges of his control begin to fray. "Enough," he said. "Not like this. I need to be inside of you. I need you."

He kissed her mouth, positioning his body over her as he laid her back on the bed, pressing himself between her legs and guiding himself inside of her.

She cried out as he filled her slowly, taking care with her innocence as he did.

He froze, the tendons in his neck standing out. His teeth clenched.

And she looked at him, this man who was trying so hard to exhibit restraint. This man who was hers and hers alone.

And the joy of that nearly burst inside her like fireworks.

He was hers. He was hers. No other woman had ever had him like this. He was inside of her. The only man she had ever been with.

What they were giving each other was beautiful, and in that moment, she thought of the woman. The woman that Cairo was bringing back here. That woman would not have this. Only she did.

She would own him forever in this way.

She shuddered as he thrust in the rest of the way, as pleasure replaced the slight pain that she felt at the invasion. As need began to ripple through her once more.

He thrust hard and fast into her, and stopped when both of them came close to their peak. He let them come down, before pushing them to the edge again. And again and again. Until she was shaking. Begging yet again. "Finish it," she said.

"I don't ever want it to end," he said.

"Please." She lifted her head up from the pillow and she kissed his mouth.

He growled, his hips pistoning forward, thrusting into her over and over again as he cried out her name, his grip bruising on her hips. "Riyaz," she shouted out his name, while his own release was a wordless exultation, another feral growl that echoed in the chamber.

And then she held him, against her body, until he reversed their positions and cradled her to his chest. "Mine," he said.

He stroked her hair, and she snuggled into his chest. And she felt the profound sense of peace like she had never felt before.

"Mine," she whispered.

Even though she knew that once this moment ended, those proclamations would be nothing more than lies.

CHAPTER SEVEN

WHEN HE WOKE in the dark, everything was soft. There was a soft mattress beneath him, and a soft woman lying against him.

His body did not hurt. He was not cold.

And he woke all the same. Yet wholly different too.

It was quite unlike anything he had ever experienced before. And for a moment, he resisted opening his eyes. Resisted rousing at all. He had never even dreamed anything this nice.

But soon, the sunshine beckoned, and when he opened his eyes, it was Brianna.

"Good morning," he said. "That was fantastic sex."

She opened her eyes, and looked at him. "That's quite a greeting."

"I do not see the point in denying what it was."

"Yes. But maybe you should work on your poetry."

"I can do that," he said, taking himself back to

books he had read. To romance. To the way that men talked to women in those books. "The heat of your body warmed me in ways nothing else ever could. But that should not surprise me. You are the sun, after all."

"I'm what?"

"The first time I saw the sun… You were standing in it."

She shifted, and he looked into her lovely face.

"What?"

"That day in the palace. I had not come upstairs yet. I had not seen the sun. It was only with you that I saw it for the first time."

"Oh. Well. That is adjacent to poetry. I am impressed."

"I do try. Or maybe not."

"Riyaz," she said. "I want to ask you something."

"And so you have to tell me you want to ask? Can you just ask?" He moved his hand over her bare arm. But he found he would rather touch her bare breast, so he did just that.

"I can't concentrate when you do that."

"Well, the question is important to you, but I did not say that it was important to me."

"Do you want any of this? Do you want to be king? Do you want to rule this country?"

"I don't understand."

"Has anyone ever asked what you wanted? Do you want to marry Ariel Hart, or is it just…? Is it just something that you were told you would do? And now that you're back on the path..."

"You must understand, that when you are royalty... What you want is not part of the conversation. Not in the same way it is in these normal houses. I read about them too. Where they ask children what they want to be when they grow up. It is a thing that you choose. That is not true when you are a royal. When you are a royal, then it is all decided for you. Before your birth. There is a line that carries back thousands of years. In many ways, it made being a prisoner easier. My job is to endure. That is all. And so I did."

"What about your happiness?"

"I have never thought about my happiness one way or the other. My appetites, certainly. But not my happiness. My job was to survive to take the throne. It is not about what I want. It never has been."

"That is very... It's very grim."

"You have accused me of this before. Perhaps it is. And yet there are far worse things in the world than being born into a purpose that you are sure of. I have never had to question anything. All that mattered was the throne. It is about the symbolism, not who I am."

"Is that how you managed to feel no... Embarrassment or shame? You're so deeply rooted in who you are. And nothing that you say or do is ever going to take that away."

"Exactly. I might have been in a dungeon, *habibti*,

but I was not the imposter. I never could be. My family's blood is in the stones of this palace. And I was always the Sheikh whether I was beneath the ground or on the throne. So asking me now…do I want to sit on the throne…? It is not really a question. I am the throne."

"But there are moments, right?" she asked softly. "Moments of happiness. Happiness matters."

"I will carry this one with me," he said, touching her face. "I will remember this."

She tightened her hold on him, clung to him rather fiercely, and he could not deny that he enjoyed that. There was not a more powerful feeling than that of having given a woman pleasure, he decided.

Yes, his own felt good. That could not be denied. But his own pleasure was easy enough to come by— the pleasure she gave him because she desired him, the pleasure that he was able to give to her, that was the sort of alchemy that created pure gold. And that was something far beyond sexual gratification.

He did not take it or her for granted.

Another thing she had taught him, he supposed.

He looked at her, and tried to imagine another woman in her place. It didn't matter what he wanted. Not really. Ariel would be the appropriate symbol. Brianna was nobody. From nowhere.

Except that she was the sun.

There was that. But the sun would always shine. One did not have to keep it locked in the palace in order for that to be true.

"This was a good lesson," he said.

She went stiff in his arms. And he realized that this was a case when honesty had not been the right choice.

"A lesson," she said.

"Yes," he responded. "Skills I will need..."

"I understood what you meant," she said. "It is only that I found it offensive. I don't need to be your lesson. And I don't understand... How you could even say that. After what we shared with one another. Doesn't that feel intimate to you?"

He wanted her. He could not imagine wanting anyone else. But she did not fit into his life, and could not.

Perhaps you could keep her. A concubine. A second wife.

He imagined showering her in gems. Wrapping her in beautiful silks. Making her the most beautiful room in the palace. He liked that.

But no matter what had passed between them...it did not change what he was. That he could hurt her. That he could hurt others around him.

She'd already had a life filled with pain. Lived in a home with a man she feared. He could not subject her to that.

"I just thought..." She got out of bed and turned to him, her expression pained. "Look, I understand that you're marrying someone else. But I didn't think that I was a *lesson* for *her.*"

"You were not only that. I'm only saying that it is perhaps valuable…"

"Don't try to dig yourself out. You're only going to make it worse. I feel… I feel like an idiot. I feel like an idiot for having trusted you with my body. I thought that it meant something to you because it was a first for you. I didn't realize that it was just… A lesson."

"You were happy for the night," he said.

"Yes. But I'm not happy now."

She dressed, quickly. And he knew that he should probably say something, but he was too captivated by the sight of her body to speak.

She turned away from him, and began to walk toward the door.

"Brianna…"

"No. You and I are through. If this is only me training you, then I cannot give you my body as part of your training. I'm not prepared to do it. I was never with a man before you. I thought that it meant something. I thought that…"

How could it mean any more than it did? He would have stayed in this bed with her gladly forever. But he *couldn't*. That was clear to him and it should be clear to her as well. He didn't know what she wanted.

And it… It enraged him. He was tired of not understanding.

He followed her out without bothering to dress. "What is your game?" he said. "You came to my bed knowing that I was to marry someone else. You know that I am the Sheikh. You know…"

"It's what you *said*," she said. "Can't you keep it separate?"

"I'm sorry," he said. "I was trying to compliment you."

"Well, it was a terrible compliment. You shouldn't try that. Just be broody and hot and good in bed. But don't try to make me feel good. You aren't good at it."

It felt just a little like she'd lodged a knife in his chest. "Am I allowed to be hurt by that?"

"That depends," she said. "*Are* you hurt by that? Are you just asking because now you want to pretend that it's even somehow?" She looked away from him. "You are naked."

"I don't care. I'm the Sheikh. Everyone should be so honored as to see the entirety of my royal visage. And if not, they can avert their gaze. It is not my job to make anyone more comfortable. They are supposed to make me comfortable."

"All those years in the dungeon, you're out for just a little while and you think that you're the only person who matters?"

"I was the only person that mattered in the dungeon. I was more free there then I am here. I had nothing and no one else to consider. Brianna, I am sorry that what I said hurt you. I have read a lot about feelings, but the thing about reading is…you see inside people's heads and I cannot see inside yours."

"Is it that you can't see inside my head, Riyaz, or is it that people in books aren't real?"

"I don't know enough about feelings," he said. "With real people, that is the truth."

"Well, word of wisdom. When you actually do have a wife, don't tell her that you learned interesting ways to pleasure her with another woman. Women don't like to hear about other women in the bedroom. Would you like it if I talked to you about other men? If I told you that it was a great lesson? And the next time that I go down on a man, he's going to benefit from what I learned from you? Maybe it will even be your brother." She turned and began to walk away from him, and he growled, grabbing hold of her arm.

"I would not like to dismember my brother, Brianna, do not tempt me to it."

"It is no less than what you said to me. Sit with it."

And then she stomped away from him down the hall, leaving him alight with fury and rage.

And another feeling that—were he not him—he might have called regret. But he was the Sheikh. Whether he was in the dungeon or not. Whether she was angry at him or not.

Nothing changed that. Nothing.

CHAPTER EIGHT

SHE WAS NUMB. She had been… Foolish. An absolute idiot. She thought about calling Cairo for another update, but what was there to say? She had done something incredibly stupid, and then she had the audacity to get angry at Riyaz for being… Whatever he was.

She had thought that he was tortured because of his time in the dungeon, but she almost wondered if he just was… *This*.

If he didn't connect to people. If he didn't feel anything.

Maybe that was why he had survived.

Maybe he had been like that before, and there was nothing more for him to get back to.

Except… She could remember when he had been all fury that day in the library. She could remember when he had held her last night. When he had made love to her with all the passion that he possessed.

He did have feelings. She knew he did. She just had no idea how it related to… The way that he attached to people. Or didn't. Was she just the same as Ariel? Did it not matter who she was?

Maybe he would just talk the way he did to anyone. Maybe that was the other side of his strange sort of honesty.

That he would simply say those things to anyone. The same that he might make love to any female body.

She had always known that Cairo was a bit like that in his sexual pursuits. The person didn't matter to him. Not in the least. It was simply about pleasure, and how he might find it. Maybe that was just some way that they were. Maybe it was in his blood, just like that right to the throne.

She went to her room, took a shower and scrubbed her skin, cried while she did, because she didn't actually want to rid herself of his touch. She had enjoyed it too much. She cared about him too much. She was angry now, but she was already beginning to question that anger. Maybe he hadn't meant anything by it. She knew that he hadn't. He didn't understand how that would hurt.

Or he didn't care.

Well, he wasn't for her. That was the thing. It was just that she had gotten caught up in the fantasy, and she had told herself that she was okay with it. She had told herself that it was all right that this wasn't going to be forever. She had told herself that she didn't want more from him. But...

She stayed away from him that day. And the next.

She didn't bother to go looking for him. When she finally came out of her room the next morning, she was told by the staff that he had not come to any meals the last days.

"Well, where is he?"

"I think he's gone back to the dungeon," one of the men said.

"Oh, for heaven's sake," she muttered.

He was having a tantrum, was what he was doing. He was angry because she was like a toy that had been taken away from him. Nothing more. So he was down in the dungeon being a misery. That was about right. That was in keeping with who he was. The kind of man that would *say* that you had given him a *great lesson*.

She gritted her teeth and before she knew it, her feet were carrying her down to the dungeon. Why couldn't she stay away from him? Why wasn't she angry enough to not care right now? She should only care about herself and her own pain and she was still drawn toward him like a magnet.

He was sitting on the bench. Staring. And then he looked up at her. "Why did you remove yourself from me?"

It was so raw and rough, so real and visceral and did he really not understand?

"Because I was *angry* at you," she said. "You're so fond of honesty, and yet when it's given to you, you don't seem to be able to understand it, and you are not a stupid man, Riyaz, so it begins to seem disingenuous. I was angry at you. *You hurt me.* You shouldn't have said what you did."

He looked her up and down, as if searching for wounds he could see.

"I am sorry," he said.

"Are you sorry because you know that it hurt me? Or sorry that you hurt me? Or are you simply sorry that I *removed myself* from you so you could not play with my body?"

"Of course I'm sorry that I could not have you again. What foolish man would not be? Yes. I want you. For more than one night. Yes, I was furious that you deprived me of your company at meals. What is the point in having them if I'm not sitting with you? I might as well go back to the dungeon."

It was… A declaration of feelings, and nothing could have surprised her more.

"Riyaz…"

"Leave me."

"No," she said. "Not until you explain this. It won't do for the Sheikh to be having tantrums in the dungeon when he is denied what he wants."

"What, then, am I supposed to do?"

"I don't know. But not go back here. This isn't yours. It was never supposed to be for you. This is for your enemies. It isn't for you."

He growled. "I know I'm not supposed to do that. I find that I don't care."

"But you care about my feelings."

"Yes, I do," he said. "I also care that if you're

angry at me you won't sleep with me. But I care about your feelings."

"Riyaz… Some of this is my fault. I wanted you to be something that you can't be. It's pointless. You can't give me what I want."

"Your normal family."

That was just the tip of the iceberg. But she wasn't going to say that to him. She wasn't going to get soft and needy now.

"Exactly. This is not the life that I want. It isn't ever going to be the life that I want. And so… Wanting you to give me something… Something more. Something romantic, I guess… It isn't especially fair. But I didn't want to think about you with her."

"Jealousy."

"Yes. Remember what I said to you about me using my skills on another man?"

He growled again.

"Exactly. It makes me want to growl too. So maybe we both know that's ahead of us. But it isn't something I wanted to hear when we were in bed."

He cupped her cheek, and without any sort of warning or preamble, he kissed her. Deep and hard and passionate. His tongue delved to the recesses of her mouth, slid against hers.

And she was powerless to do anything but return the kiss.

Because he was glorious.

Because she wanted him, no matter that he had infuriated her. Because she cared for him.

Because her chest was a tangled-up mess, and she didn't want anyone or anything else.

"Have me here," he growled. "You had me in a bed. That is your world. Have me in this world. This is why. This is why I am *me*."

Because no matter that he was the Sheikh in either place, it had affected him. She heard that. Unspoken in that hoarse plea. And she was powerless to resist.

She stripped his shirt off, just as he did the same to hers. She had on a skirt, thank God, so while she was undoing the closure on his pants, he had swept her underwear to the side, and when she rose up on his lap, and down onto his hardened arousal, she gasped as he filled her.

It didn't matter that there was no foreplay. She was wet. From his kiss. From the ever-present need for him that she carried around with her at all times.

She began to ride him. And each thrust of her hips over his was a declaration. Was possessive. Possession.

She claimed him, over and over again, and when he gripped the back of her head and tugged her hair tight, fastening his mouth to hers, she was claimed yet again.

How could there ever be anyone else?

Except there had to be. Because they were from two different worlds. And she didn't want his.

And he had someone else in mind for him.

She shuddered out her climax, and he roared his

own. And they clung together in the aftermath, in the dark, in the dungeon.

He rested his head against her collarbone. "That is good," he said. "That I was able to have you in this place. It healed something in me."

"What if we went to the garden?" she whispered. "Have you been outside yet?"

He kissed her neck. "Not yet."

She nodded. She understood. There were certain things that were going to take time.

Of course, what she did not expect was for that time to be dramatically shortened when a holy man from the country arrived at the palace.

"I have just come from the desert. And I have no wish to cause anyone harm or distress, but I am compelled to give you honesty. Your brother, Cairo, has married your fiancée."

She could see a black rage come over Riyaz. And her heart broke in two.

Ariel had married someone else. And that choice had been taken from him. It was only a few moments later that it registered to her that… Cairo was married. Cairo, whom she had fancied herself in love with before the beginning of all of this.

It was a moment of brutal clarity. She wasn't in love with Cairo anymore. The hurt here was that… Riyaz would never be able to choose her over Ariel. Because Ariel had been taken from him.

You idiot girl. You don't want him to choose you.

You don't want to stay here. What kind of a life is this? With a man like him.

"Brianna," he said. "We must go to the desert."

"Riyaz, you haven't even been outside yet," she said.

"It is of no consequence," he said. "I decree that we shall, and therefore we shall. The desert will bend to my will."

And that was how she found herself in a helicopter, clinging to the seat for all she was worth. She didn't like this. Not at all. Her breath was coming in short, sharp gasps, panic making itself known in every facet of her body. Completely uncontrollable.

And there was something about the way he was right now. Wild. Untamed. And she didn't know what to make of any of it.

He was clearly in a jealous rage, over his brother marrying a woman that he hadn't even seen for sixteen years. It made it obviously how little what had happened between herself and Riyaz mattered to him at all.

But also, she had a vague concern that Riyaz meant to shed Cairo's blood. Cairo was supposed to be the one that she was in love with. That was the thing. Cairo was supposed to be the one who mattered.

He was the one who had saved her. He was the one that she had thought herself to be in love with. And she had no idea what any of that meant now.

When her body still ached with the memory of Riyaz's touch.

Well, her body did not ache now. It was trembling.

Helicopters really were terrible.

Riyaz, for his part, was stone. Motionless. Showing no emotion as they flew quickly over the desert. As he experienced this sort of freedom for the first time in all those years.

It was like he had shut all that off. Like none of it mattered.

And maybe the way that he compartmentalized all these things with such brutal efficiency was part of how he had survived, but she found it… Jarring. Painful. And then, even with her eyes partway closed, she saw beneath the helicopter, a tent. Out in the middle of the golden desert sand.

"Here," Riyaz said to the pilot. The helicopter lowered suddenly, and in spite of herself, Brianna clung to Riyaz's arm. Her anxiety had no pride.

And when the helicopter touched down, Riyaz stepped out onto the desert sand. And she couldn't help but feel something momentous well inside of her. Because there he was, out on the sands as he was meant to be. As he had not been all this time. And he strode toward the tent, with Brianna scrambling after him. "Riyaz," she said. "Please don't do anything…"

And then he opened the flap of the tent, and Brianna saw Cairo in the flesh for the first time in weeks. He was standing there looking ready to do

battle himself. And she waited. To feel something.
For Cairo.

Instead, all she felt was terror.

"And here I find you. With my woman," said
Riyaz.

"My apologies," said Cairo. "She is no longer
yours. I have married her. And we have consum-
mated it. Quite thoroughly. You will find."

"So I see." He looked around the tent, his gaze as-
sessing. And she worried… She could feel the energy
vibrating off of him and remembered the way that he
had come apart in the library. Brianna touched his
arm, and he stiffened beneath her fingers, then…he
came back to himself. "What is it?" he asked, looking at her.

"You don't want to kill your brother," she said.

He took her chin in his hand, the hold possessive, his dark gaze intense. "I know that, *habibti*. I
don't intend to." Then he turned back to Cairo, and
she could feel his rage again. "The dungeon might
be suitable."

"The dungeon. Is that what you think?" she asked,
her heart pounding wildly.

"And will you throw Ariel there as well?" Cairo
asked.

"I am the Sheikh. I could marry her if I chose,
regardless of whether or not she is bound to you."
He paused. "Or I could throw her in there with you.
Or… Take two wives."

"Two wives?" Cairo asked.

"Yes," he said. "For I have already decided who I will marry."

Brianna felt the tent tilt.

"You said that you wanted to marry her," Cairo said, gesturing to Ariel.

"I said for you to bring her to me. I said it was what I required. I did not say why. I had thought that I might marry her. But I have decided on another course of action."

"What is that?" Cairo asked.

"I'm marrying Brianna."

And the world became nothing more than shattered glass.

"Riyaz…"

"It will be no argument," he said. "You are mine. Or have I not made you so these last days?"

Brianna's face went hot and she knew Cairo would know, immediately, what had happened between herself and Riyaz.

Their passion was incendiary, but marriage? He had never once acted like he wanted anything but sex from her.

"The situation is complicated, I see," Cairo said. "How dare you burst into my wedding tent given that you already decided what you plan to do?"

"I have not said yes," said Brianna, and then she rounded on Riyaz. "I'm not yours. I don't live here. I'm not a citizen of this country I don't…"

"You're mine now," he said. "Our bodies do not lie. You have lain with me, and you will be my wife."

Brianna's whole body felt like it was on fire. "Can you please not announce…?"

"You have stormed into the aftermath of my wedding night," Cairo said directly to her. "Why should you be embarrassed to have your own activities commented upon?"

"Cairo," she said. "I'm sorry. I…"

"You know, both of you could ask the women around you what they want," Ariel said. "Just because a woman sleeps with you it does not mean she wishes to marry you. Just because she is born doesn't mean she wishes to marry you. Just because her father says."

"Yes," said Brianna. "Exactly that."

"It is done," said Cairo. "You are my wife."

"I'm not *his* wife," said Brianna.

Riyaz looked her up and down. "You will be. Perhaps we might find someone our here to do the deed."

Panic rolled through her.

"You cannot get married in a desert," said Cairo. "You must have a wedding that is symbolic for the people."

"You do not get to order me around. I have spent enough time in captivity."

"But are not concerned at all about putting others in captivity," said Ariel. "I'm pleased that you're alive, Riyaz," she said. "But it doesn't give you license to act like a monster."

"Monster or not. You're both coming with me.

Back to Nazul. These games have gone on long
enough. It is time I begin my rule."

And that was how they all ended up back in the
helicopter. And Brianna felt absolutely shamefaced
sitting next to Cairo, with Riyaz across from her, and
the very delicate and beautiful Ariel by him.

She couldn't even bring herself to feel anxious
about the helicopter ride this time. There was too
much else that was going on.

Marriage.

She would lose everything. Her dreams for a normal life. She had loved Cairo all this time and never
made a move toward him because she'd known he
couldn't give her what she wanted.

Her sweet little family home. Her sweet little family life.

And now Riyaz thought she could marry him?
Live in a palace? Be…royalty? How?

*You did touch him. You never really wanted Cairo.
Not like this. Not like you want him.*

But why was Riyaz even doing this? To save face
after Cairo had taken his fiancée from him?

What was worse? Being forced into marriage and
losing her last grasp on her idyllic, simple-life fantasy?

Or being forced to marry a man who was only
doing it to get back at his brother?

It didn't take long for them to get back to Nazul.
For them to get back to the palace.

"Go into the palace," Riyaz said. "I will follow you there."

The helicopter went away, and Brianna stood beside him as he simply lingered, there in the desert. She watched as the sun touched his face, and even in her fury at him, she recognized the moment. His freedom. This first time just being. Outside. In the light.

"Riyaz... You cannot demand that I marry you."

"Certainly I can. You are here. And I am the Sheikh."

"Riyaz... You were held prisoner in a dungeon. You would do the same thing to me?"

"The whole world makes demands of you that you do not wish. And this... It is not a dungeon."

And then he turned and walked back into the palace, leaving her there to marinate on her fate.

"How dare you make war with me when you have taken my friend—who I told you was fragile, and you have..."

Riyaz waved a hand, cutting his brother off. "Do not speak to me in such a way. You seem to think that because you lived on the outside for all of these years that you know more than I do. That you get to make commands. Dictating what you believe to be the right thing from your position. You have pulled the strings on all of this, as you have sought to pull the strings on me."

"That is a lie. Everything that I have done has

been for your benefit. Except for this. I want her. And I have wanted her from the beginning." Cairo's voice went rough. "I have… I have cared for her since I was a child. And it is… It felt a betrayal to me then. And a folly. And I could not control that which I wanted from her. When she was with me I… I found that I could not give her to you. She could only ever be mine."

And Riyaz did not want her. He did not want two wives. He wanted Brianna, and there was no scope for anything else. No scope for anyone else. And he did not know why he hadn't made that declaration in the first place.

It was only her. Only Brianna.

Would you do the same thing to me?

It wasn't the same. And anyway. Had he not been denied enough? He would have her. He would keep her. He would give her more than she had ever been given. And perhaps… Perhaps this had been a big disappointment to her. Cairo marrying another woman. He would keep her from disappointment.

"Are you going to kill me?" Cairo asked.

"No. Enough blood has been shed in these halls. I am deeply uninterested in killing you over a woman that I do not want. I want Brianna."

"Does Brianna want you?"

"She seems to want me well enough when she is naked with me."

Cairo seemed to dislike that statement.

"She did not seem particularly like she wishes to marry you, though."

He waved his hand. "Neither did Ariel. Did she wish to marry you?"

"That's different."

"Why? Because Brianna is your friend, and you feel possessive of her?" Riyaz asked.

"Did you only decide to have her to get at me? Was she collateral?"

"Do you love her?"

"No," said Cairo, frowning. "Not like you mean."

"She loves you."

He hated that she did, but she'd said it herself, and why should Cairo not know it?

"She doesn't really. She idolizes me because I rescued her. It is not the same."

"It is. She would've chosen you. Though... She cannot resist me. These are inconvenient things. Bodies. I have had no prior experience with it. It is... Intoxicating."

"Marry her then," Cairo said. "But you must have a ceremony that gives the country hope. And you cannot have a bride that looks as though she is being forced."

"I will handle it. And there will be no consequence for you and Ariel. It is also a good thing, I think," he said slowly. "Yes. It is a good thing. Her marrying you or me... The end result is the same. It puts to right something that was wrong. It does not allow her father to have the final say, and it… It may heal something. For our people."

"You are not quite so far gone as you allowed me to believe."

"I was," he said. "Brianna is remarkable."

It was no less than the truth.

"We will announce your marriage, and my up-coming nuptials before the people. I will appear before them for the first time." He nodded. "Yes. This is the way. It will be an excellent first appearance."

"You should get a haircut," said Cairo.

"No. There are certain things about my experience that I cannot erase. And there are certain things that I choose to keep. I will never be the king that our father was. After what I've been through, it's impossible. But I will work to win back every single year that I lost. Every single year we all lost. I will be the ruler this country needs. On that you can trust me. Now. There are apartments set aside for you and your wife. Apartments fitting the new head of the military. We all have our responsibilities."

Cairo looked at him, hard. "Do you love her?"

Everything inside of Riyaz rejected that. Rejected anything like it. He had to keep his emotions more stable than that. He was a potential danger, he knew.

That was why.

He had to protect her. So he had to be in control of himself.

"I don't love," said Riyaz. "But I want her. And I will have her. And you… You won't stop me."

"You're right," said Cairo. "I won't. Because I have the woman that I want… You should have the woman you want."

"So cheaply you sell your friend. The woman who loves you."

"Do you intend to hurt her?"

Riyaz thought about it. He knew that he didn't want to, but he had to consider the possibility that he could. He had very nearly done so in the library.

"No," he said. The idea of hurting her was anathema to him.

"Very well," said Cairo. "But my conscience is clear. As long as you will care for her. Keep her safe…"

"I swear my life on it. I will do whatever needs doing in order to make her happy."

"Good."

"There is a room prepared for you in the back of the palace. It will be your quarters. And you will remember your place."

"It would probably do you well to remember yours," said Cairo. "You are a figurehead, and an imperfect one. And we will need to announce my marriage and yours, and you will have to be ready to face the nation."

"I am ready," said Riyaz.

"Are you?"

"Brianna will make sure that I am. Whenever you say I should."

"You put a lot on your fiancée."

Riyaz nodded. He couldn't deny that he did. "Because she is strong."

And that was the truest thing of all.

CHAPTER NINE

THE NEXT DAY was a whirlwind. They made plans to make the announcement of his engagement, and of Cairo's marriage to Ariel.

Brianna had spent Ariel's first moments of the palace with her, and over the next few days, she found herself with the other woman quite a bit. She wasn't jealous. But she also wasn't fully resigned to the idea of marrying Riyaz either. But then… She wasn't sure she knew what she wanted. At all. She couldn't imagine leaving Riyaz altogether. But at the same time… She had wanted a normal life.

This would be the furthest thing from that. She wasn't certain she could handle that.

"Apparently we're announcing my marriage to Cairo today," said Ariel.

"You've been prepared to marry one of them your whole life. I guess that must feel… Like it was coming this whole time?"

Ariel shook her head. "I wouldn't say that. No. I wouldn't say that. I have loved Cairo since I was a girl. But I spent a long while thinking that he was dead. I didn't think that he had survived, and even if he had, I didn't think I would ever see him again. Much less be married to him. I knew that I didn't want Riyaz. Not ever. We met and there was just no… Connection. I was miserable here at the palace except when I was with Cairo. But you know, the years passed, and things become complicated. He was different when he was a boy."

"But you love him still."

"And you?"

"Yes," said Brianna, honestly. "But as a friend. I thought for a time that I might want him. Because he was the kindest, most wonderful man I had ever known. Because he was a man who cared for me without wanting anything in return. Because that felt revolutionary for a very long time in my life. Especially considering where I come from. I wanted him to love me, because I thought maybe we could heal each other. Maybe we could find something normal and wonderful and special together. But we can't. And I recognize that now. Because… Because he's my friend. He's not the love of my life."

"Is Riyaz?"

That question terrified her. She genuinely didn't want to answer to it. Because if he was the love of her life then… What did that mean for anything? For her life, for her own sanity.

How could she want this? A life in this palace,

with that man, who she felt was fundamentally broken in some way.

And even as she thought that, she had an image of wanting to hold him together. Wanting to keep him from shattering into more pieces.

Did anyone know her as well as he did? In just these few days, had anyone ever gotten to know her in a way that was any deeper? Any more real?

She already knew the answer to that.

"Riyaz is complicated. It's like he… Imprinted on me. For lack of a better word. I was the first woman that he saw when he came out of the dungeon. I don't know if he knows what he wants."

"If he is anything like Cairo, then he absolutely knows what he wants. He's already decided. And woe to the rest of us."

"Yes. I believe that to be true in terms of what he wants to possess. But whether or not he has any idea what he feels? Or if it's all just… Well. Stockholm syndrome."

"You think he has it with you?" Ariel laughed. "I was a bit worried that I had it with Cairo. But if so, then I've had it since I was fourteen. Is it Stockholm syndrome? Or is it just powerful feelings expanded by close proximity, by the intensity of the situation? Maybe it makes it faster, but maybe they would've been there regardless."

There was something oddly comforting about Ariel's words. But then, Ariel wasn't in a situation that was any more conventional than Brianna's. So maybe it was just what the other woman had to think in order to feel comforted about her own marriage.

Why aren't you allowed to be comforted? Maybe you should be allowed to feel all right about the situation you're in. Because you wanted it. Regardless of what you've ever told yourself about wanting a normal life, you want this.

That made her want to wail in anger. That maybe she was just too messed up, too broken, to actually even want something normal. She had an image in her mind, but maybe she couldn't even actually aspire to that because of everything that she was.

Her connection to Cairo hadn't fixed her. And it had led right here. And maybe that was the real issue.

"There are worse things, you know," Ariel said, "than having a beautiful, powerful man be a little bit obsessed with you."

"Yes, but this beautiful, powerful man is so intense sometimes I think he might burn me alive. And he says things that… He says things that hurt sometimes."

"Well. That's not ideal. And I guess him not caring about your choice isn't particularly ideal either."

He knows what I want.

That truth echoed in her chest.

And it made her feel horrifically uncomfortable.

He did know what she wanted. And deep down, she did too. She wanted him. She wanted for this to be something more than it was.

And she was willing to live with whatever that looked like.

She wasn't sure if she should call herself a fool, or praise her determination.

She really wasn't sure at all.

And yet she knew, that whatever she said or did, her marriage was being announced today, without her being present for that announcement.

And she had to decide what she was going to do in response to that. She had to find a way to exert her own will.

Because Riyaz actually wouldn't even respect her otherwise.

They had done it. That stereotypical balcony announcement. Riyaz had managed to make a speech promising to bring the country together. And Cairo had announced his marriage to Ariel, and declared it a unifying marriage, that would heal the past betrayals of the country.

It had been a masterful expression of public relations, if Riyaz said so himself.

And it was quite different than anything he had ever done before. And really, everything he believed in. Hadn't he told Brianna multiple times that he didn't understand why people were so dishonest? About what they wanted and who they were. And yet, here he was playing a part of his first official act as ruler of the country. But maybe that was the point of all of this.

Except, when he had chosen Brianna to be his

wife, it had nothing to do with the public face of anything. It had to do with what he wanted. In his room. In his bed. But, of course, he was now in this role, and he had to learn to play it.

Even if the entire exercise seemed pointless to him.

He had spent these last days preparing for this announcement with his brother. He had not had Brianna in his bed.

In part because… He was not entirely certain that she would have him. Not after the way his proposal had been received.

Perhaps it had been less a proposal and more of a demand. And yet, he wanted her. But wanting her felt so separate to this new phase he found himself in. This one where he did have to strive to put on a face for the public sometimes. Because now they knew… Now they knew he was back.

They knew that he was not dead.

And again, in some strange way, he felt his freedom slipping away from him.

Because now he was owned by a nation.

When before he had only had to answer to himself.

He had only ever stepped outside that one day into the desert. And then again onto the balcony.

But he had not gone out… Just for himself.

And that was how he found himself, in the late afternoon, stepping out into the beautiful courtyard garden. All white walls and mosaic. It was fragrant, just like he remembered from his childhood. Jasmine, orange blossoms and gardenia.

The air was thick with it.

And right by the fountain at the center, he saw Brianna. She was sitting there wearing a white dress, her shoulders exposed, her red hair like a copper curtain flowing over her shoulders, covering her face.

"Brianna," he said. She looked up at him, and his heart stopped. And all he could think about was how he wanted her. Was that even surrounded by all of this beauty, like that which he had not seen for years, she was still the most beautiful, the rarest site of all. The most stunning beauty.

"What are you doing out here?"

"I came to see the courtyard, but that you are here too feels… Right. We are to be married in eight days," he said.

"Oh, are we? You know, normally, you have to check the bride's availability for the wedding."

"You know how it is between us."

"How what is? That you need a wife, and I happened to be standing there, not married to your brother, so it seemed like I was a decent option?"

"No," he said. "You know that what we feel for one another is undeniable."

"You're talking about sex. Attraction."

"Yes. I am. But as you and I have both never given in to that attraction with anyone else, it is significant."

"Slightly more significant for the person who

hasn't spent the last sixteen years in a dungeon," she said.

He looked at her. Honestly trying to figure out why she was pushing at him. Pushing against him and this. Was it that sitcom family she wanted? She was a smart enough woman to know that whatever a person wanted from their life, they were not guaranteed to get it. That did not mean all was lost. And he should know.

"I lived sixteen years in a dungeon. You lived fifteen with a man who did not care for you at all. We have both experienced long stretches of life that were unfair. That were not what we had would've chosen. Is it not good enough to feel this desire?"

"I don't know," she said, feeling choked. "I don't know what I'm supposed to want anymore."

"Who cares what we are supposed to do?" And in fact, he didn't want to think about supposed to.

He wanted to get back to elemental. Back to what felt right. Back to what made sense. He wanted to get back to that space where there was honesty. Where that was what mattered.

And here he was, out in the sun, free to be for the first time in so many years.

"Do you not know," he said. "All that matters is this feeling. This is real. You would trade it for something you may never be able to have? For a man in khaki pants who complains to you about his job, who leaves the dishes for you to do, who makes you feel as if you must do unequal work caring for

your children? That is this *normal* that you want? It
is what you crave?"

"No. Of course not."

"What we have found, it is something other than
normal. It is honest, at least. Honest in its intensity.
In all that we are. It is the truth. And can we at least
live in truth if we cannot live in the reality that we
have chosen? All of that… All that I must be when
standing on a balcony giving a speech to my people,
it is not the truth. It is what they need to see. A marriage to Ariel would have been what they needed to
see. But I wish to marry you for all that we are when
we are not in front of people."

And he would keep her safe. From himself. He
would keep himself under control, and keep her with
him.

He could do both.

He was resolved.

And he had not yet failed when he was resolved.

"Really?"

"Yes," he said. "You make me feel like there is no
end to the heat that we can create. And that… That
is simply ours. It does not belong to anyone else. For
so many years my life was only mine. Well, with the
exception that I could not choose to leave the dungeon. But within that dungeon, it was mine. Ever
since leaving, it has been so much more about what
others want from me. And this is a hazard of being
born the Sheikh. But it has been a change. If I am to
survive all of this, it is not simply about you teach-

ing me how to behave. It is about you giving me a space where I do not have to. And what about you, Brianna? Who are you apart from all of this? Who are you apart from all these demands you place on yourself? You teach people to be civilized. Perhaps I should teach you how to be wild."

He could see conflict in her eyes. He hated that these moments between them were all conflict.

He crossed the space to her, and pulled her up into his arms. "I am outside. Beneath the sky and the sun, because I can be. And I would have you naked. Out here. Because we can. And damn everyone else. Damn everything else. Yes, there is much twisting and contorting for all of this. For all the people in there. For all the people out there. But here we are, just the two of us. What will we make it? Will you allow yourself to be wild? Will you allow this fire to burn your skin?"

"To what end?" She sounded sad, desperate.

"To feel," he said. "To feel all of the things that we weren't allowed to."

And that seemed to spark something in her. Desire. Madness. Something. Because then she wrapped her arms around his neck, and kissed him. Deep and hard, the desert sun exacerbating the heat between them.

Bringing it to a raging inferno.

"You will be my wife," he said.

"Yes," she whispered, sounding broken.

"We do not need to be a sitcom, Brianna. We are

wild. And we have already been held captive. Why should we continue to hold ourselves prisoner?"

And then she began to tear at his clothes. As if she was desperate to remove any barriers between them. Or remove the last vestiges of civility. He knew that he was.

For this was freedom. Here in the blazing sun. This was perhaps who they might've been if they had not been forced to be anything else.

"Habibti," he said, his voice harsher as she reached down and wrapped her fingers around his raging arousal. He wanted this. Wanted her more than anything.

And he knew that things were not settled between them. That while she might marry him, there was work yet to be done. Miles to be traveled on a road where they could find something companionable between them.

There would always be a wall up within him. There would have to be.

For her own good.

But they both wanted this, now. But she felt that desire to be with him now. But he had been right when he had said she needed to release hold on those chains. And she was expressing that freedom in the same way that he wished to. Which meant that he was right about more than he was wrong about. And with her, that was all that mattered.

"Show me," he said, his voice hoarse. "Show me what you would do if there were no bonds. If there were no restraints. You are that wild thing that survived a childhood with a crime lord for a father. Be that wild thing. Show me what you are."

She grabbed his face, and kissed him, and then she raked her nails down his chest, the pain searing and arousing all at once.

"Yes," he growled. "Give me everything."

She moved her hips against his, her desire as insistent as his own. And he put his hand there, and found her slick and wet with wanting.

She gasped out his name but it wasn't enough. He wanted more. He wanted everything.

Because they had been in chains. Not just during their time when they were held captive, but in this time when they were trying to rejoin the world. They had muzzled themselves. And they had… They had it difficult. Figuring out what was real, what was wrong and what was innately part of what they were.

And so now… Now… They were owed freedom.

He pushed two fingers inside of her. "Come for me," he growled.

She ground her hips against his hand, and she shattered.

And he didn't see the point in holding back. The point in pretending that the roar that was building inside of him wasn't there. He was not civilized. And he never would be.

Not with her. She was his, his.

And maybe that did make him as bad as the people who had held him captive. Just maybe.

But it was worth it. To have her.

For the stolen moment in the garden. All blistering heat and sunlight, and all the things that he had been denied.

Why should he be denied? Why should he experience self-denial ever again?

He shouldn't. He should have all that he wanted and more.

Everything.

He should have her. And she wanted it too, whether she could admit that or not. She claimed she wanted normal, but she didn't know what normal was.

Neither did he.

They had no metric for that. No instruction manual. They only had what they were. And what he was, was broken.

But she made him feel like shattered might not be the worst thing a man could be. He laid her back on the edge of the fountain. He reached the side and let his palm capture some of the cool water coming from the spout. And he let it drip over her breasts, watched as her nipples tightened into impossibly glorious pink beads.

"Raspberry," he growled. He leaned forward and captured her nipple between his lips. Sucked deep and hard.

Yes. She was everything he had imagined from that first moment. Tart and sweet and her. All that he needed. Everything.

His body throbbed with the need to possess her, but he did not want this to go too quickly. He wanted to savor this. To savor her. He wanted…

She was panting, begging, her hips shifting restlessly, as if she was seeking something only he could give her.

It was true.

"You might want a normal life," he said, his voice rough. "But where will you get this? Maybe we are lucky to not have normal. Maybe we are meant to have more. Maybe we are meant to be everything. The sun. The desert. The extreme. Why be a cul-de-sac when you can be the wilderness?"

"Are you going to keep talking," she panted. "Because I'm desperate for you."

"I knew that you were," he said. His need was ferocious. It had him at the edge of sanity. But then, maybe he already was. And maybe there was no fixing that, but she wanted him. And if she wanted him, it wasn't so bad.

If she wanted him, then maybe it would be all right.

Maybe he would trash the library and she would bring him cupcakes. Maybe he would create terror in the middle of the night, and she would soothe him with a movie.

And what would he give to her?

This.

This. And it would have to be enough.

He took another palm full of water and left droplets over her skin. Her breasts, her stomach. She gasped as the cold water rolled down between her legs.

She groaned, moving her hips restlessly, because he knew that she was hungry for more. More than a tease. She wanted his touch.

But this was what he had to offer her, and he had to prove that it was something beyond that which she could achieve on her own or with any other man.

This was what he had.

And he would give it to her with both hands. But he would also withhold. Because that would make it all the sweeter.

"Monster," she panted.

"When did I ever give you the impression I was anything but a monster? I think you know this to be true about me."

"Riyaz…"

"They call me the Mad Sheikh. Do you not think it's for a reason?"

"This is too calculated for you to be mad."

"Maybe. Maybe I'm just a beast."

And that was when he lowered his head between her thighs, devouring her. She gripped his head, holding him there as he feasted on her like she was a delicacy. Like she was all he could ever hope to have and more.

She dug her heels into his flanks as he did. Short, sharp sounds of need escaping her.

"Yes," he growled against her tender flesh.

She had come for him once, but he would demand that she do it again and again before he was satisfied.

He pushed two fingers inside of her again, joining with his teeth and lips and tongue, driving them both to the brink. To the edge of sanity.

And then he felt her break. Shatter. Her cries echoing off the walls in the garden.

He lifted his head and licked his lips. "Better than chocolate," he said.

She shivered. "Riyaz. Please."

He thrust inside of her finally. And she let out a hoarse cry. He moved slowly at first, doing his best to keep himself reined in. Under tight control.

He would pleasure her again. He would pleasure her again before taking his own.

She was shivering, shaking as he drew out each and every thrust. Luxuriating in the feel of it. The feel of her. And then his own control fractured. Shattered. Just as she cried out her pleasure.

And his movements became harsh, erratic. He thrust into her, again and again. As need grabbed him by the throat and shook him around. He was no longer in control. It was this. Only this. He wanted her. Needed her. Craved her beyond all else.

He gripped her hips and thrust hard, pouring himself inside of her on one last roar.

And then she came again too, her internal muscles pulsing around his arousal.

"Mine," he said. And he leaned in and kissed her lips. "You need me," he said. "You need this. For without me… Who will make you feel this way? No one. You cannot trade this for suburban despair."

"I already said I'm not leaving," she said, putting her palm flat on his chest. "I won't."

But there was a strange note in her voice, and it felt like something beginning to unravel.

He could not put his finger on it. He could not say what it was or why.

All he knew was that this moment was a temporary fix.

This moment was a Band-Aid.

It had not been the decisive thing that he had wanted it to be.

He felt disquiet in his soul, there beneath the burning sun.

"How does it feel to be out here?" she asked, sitting up slowly, drawing her knees to her chest.

He didn't know why she was asking him that. Why she was looking at him as if she felt worried.

"It is fine. When I'm with you."

"I'm glad."

"How was it for you?" He gripped her chin and forced her to look at him. She did that. Asked him how he felt. Said it was good. Said she was glad. He didn't understand. She seemed to say such bland things. In these moments. Turn them around to him. And he didn't know what the alternative was. He only knew there was something else that should be happening.

What are you to her?

And maybe that was the problem. That even he knew that this… As much as he wanted it to be, might not be enough.

He would figure it out. He would find a way to make this enough for her.

"Will we sleep in the same bed tonight?"

He considered that. "Probably not."

And she looked sad.

But he was keeping her safe. He was keeping himself on a leash, he would have to. It was the only way they could be together.

He was what he was.

He could have her. But he could only give her so much.

CHAPTER TEN

THE PREPARATION FOR a royal wedding was intense. And they were trying to make a gesture, a statement, to the entire nation, and indeed the entire world. Which made the preparations even more intense than they would have been if circumstances were normal. Not that Brianna could quite figure out what would constitute as normal for a royal wedding. All she saw was extravagance. Extravagance on a grand scale.

The dresses that were brought in for her were glorious. Made of fabrics that were so rich and luxurious she didn't think she had ever touched anything like them. Much less had them resting against her skin.

The menu that they were working on was enough to make any foodie stand up and cheer. And she couldn't deny that she was looking forward to it.

The decorations and flowers promised to be a spectacle, and looking at beautiful arrangements had been a lovely way to pass one of the days.

If only things with Riyaz were quite as straightforward as the wedding planning. They didn't share a room or a bed. He was still a part-time dungeon dweller, and given what had happened the time he had tried to sleep in a bed, she wasn't entirely sure how to convince him that it would be okay.

She wasn't even sure if it would be okay. That made it all difficult.

To make matters worse, Ariel, who had become a friend, was clearly going through some things with Cairo, and that made her a bit distant in ways that Brianna could definitely understand. "He's withdrawn," she said. "He won't sleep with me."

"Neither will Riyaz," Brianna said.

"It's this place," said Ariel. "He was different. At the house we married at. I think being here is destructive. There are too many ghosts."

But Brianna understood that there was nothing to be done about that. How could there be? They were the rulers of these ghosts. Of the people in this country. Of all that was good, and all that was dangerous, all that was sad and all that was brilliant. This place, the site of their trauma, was a place that they had to stay.

And as much she appreciated that it was difficult for Cairo, she also found herself having a difficult time being sympathetic to him. Considering that Riyaz had been here the entire time. In a dungeon. This might be Cairo's first time facing these sorts of demons, but Riyaz had been trapped in them.

And now sometimes she felt trapped in them as well. In that sense, she could well relate to Ariel.

But Riyaz was not distant. In fact, he was as attentive as could be expected. During the day, he was being given a million administrative tasks to do, things that were very unlike his life for the past sixteen years, and he was taking them all on admirably.

She imagined that he was extremely grateful that he had made it his goal to keep his mind sharp while he was imprisoned. Because there was definitely a heavy demand on his intellect now.

Thankfully, there was not yet a heavy demand on his diplomacy.

There would be eventually. Eventually, there would be meetings with dignitaries from around the world. Ambassadors and other leaders.

And he would have her.

She tried to imagine that. She had never really wanted a life like this. She had wanted something smaller.

But…

Now it was difficult to imagine a life that didn't revolve around him. So maybe it wasn't so bad. Maybe different was okay.

She walked into the ballroom, which was beginning to be set for the wedding party. The ceremony would take place outside in one of the courtyards. In the ballroom there would be dancing. Various banquet halls feasts, and outside there would be tables laden with food as well.

It would be a time of celebration for everybody.

And she couldn't help but wonder how Riyaz would feel about that.

He seemed determined to go forward with all of this and not feel anything.

The thought stopped her cold.

Maybe that was part of her own disquiet.

Riyaz handled everything much better than she ever could've imagined. But he also seemed… Cold. Distant in a way. As if he was cut off from everything. And maybe that was the only way he could get through it. Maybe it wasn't fair to think that it might be a problem.

After all, when his emotions had gotten close to the surface she had seen what happened.

His PTSD episodes had come when he was pushed too far. And maybe to protect himself from that he had to stay extra detached during these first weeks of his official rule.

Maybe that was all it was.

That thought carried her toward his study. Where she knew that he would be working now.

The throne room was ceremonial. He liked the library for certain things. But for heavy paperwork, she knew that he did like the desk that his father had once done his work at.

She wandered through the glittering palace, looking around at all of the beauty.

Yes. There were ghosts here. But more than that, there was history. There was something beautiful about this place, even if there was darkness here as well.

There was something special about it. Even if it was challenging.

All was contained here. The good and the bad.

The betrayal, the tragedy, but the love that had been here as well.

She could feel it all right then.

She wished that she had known his mother. He could barely speak about her. And she knew that meant that he had loved her very much. Because it hurt too bad to talk about her.

She could understand that.

I care about your son. Very much. I just want you to know.

She said that silent thought, that near prayer out into the universe. And then she looked at him.

"How is everything?"

"Good," he said.

"You're not working too hard, are you?"

"I don't think so."

"Would you have any idea what working too hard was?"

"I might. Are you playing the part of nagging wife in a sitcom?"

He asked it with humor, and she took it that way.

"Maybe. Is that so bad if my nagging is about your well-being?"

He shrugged. "Perhaps not."

She looked around the office and she saw that in

the corner, there was one of his spy novels that he liked. She picked it up and sat in the chair next to the desk.

"What are you doing?"

"I thought I might read. While you work."

"Did you?"

"I don't really have anything to do. And you know, I'm going to need something to do."

"We will have children," he said.

Of course they would. And of course he would expect that, and it wasn't as if they had been having protected sex, but the idea made something slam hard into her chest. Probably her heart. Or maybe every single one of her internal organs, really.

She'd wanted children, of course. It was part of that fantasy. Of picket fences and of neighborhood evenings where kids rode their bikes around until the porch lights came on.

But they didn't live in a neighborhood, and they didn't have a picket fence.

They were in the desert, with great stone walls surrounding a palace.

He was a sheikh. She was a woman whose father hadn't cared about her at all. He was a man who'd basically raised himself in a dungeon.

She wanted it, but she felt sad.

That they weren't what she'd dreamed.

She wondered if she even could be.

Children. She wanted them. Wanted his children.

She wondered what that meant for them both, but didn't want to dissolve right now.

"Of course. But that… Surely I'll have responsibilities other than the children?"

"Yes," he relented. "I suppose so."

"One thing that is quite important to me is that I have something to do with myself. Something that's my own. Having lived the kind of life that I did before I left my father's house… You can understand."

"What was it like?"

He was looking at her with intent, interest. "Well," she said, frowning slightly. "It was a huge house, often full of his cronies. It was organized crime, but I'm not sure what all… I don't want to know, I never have."

"I can understand. I understand what it's like to… to need to curate your world. Your thoughts. I had to do that in the dungeon."

She nodded slowly. "Well, I wasn't in a dungeon. I was in a big, beautiful house, with no love at all. A big, beautiful house where all of the men were monsters. I had a room, but I slept with the door locked. I had to…make myself a prisoner, in many ways."

"That's a terrible way for anyone to live. Before… before all of this. Before the takeover of the country, I had a family. A real family."

She looked away. "I never did."

"You can have one here." He cleared his throat.

"And what is family to you, Riyaz?"

"A distant memory. But I will keep you safe."

"Do you…your feelings…"

"I have to keep my control. You understand." And though neither of them said anything about love, she could tell that it had been the topic. She'd asked. He'd said no. "I thought you were going to read."

"I thought it was a good opportunity to…to talk about expectations." Her heart was thundering hard. "Because, of course, I have decided to marry you."

A small smile lifted the corner of his mouth. "It would be awkward if not, considering the wedding is fast approaching."

"Yes," she said. "I suppose that's true."

"You know as the Sheikha, you can be in charge of any number of things. Just tell me what would make you happy. You can head up any cause that you would like. That is a common thing, is it not? For the spouses of those ruling the country."

"Yes," she agreed. "It is. So, I will find something that matters to me and set up a foundation."

"Yes," he said.

Something ached inside of her chest, but she opted to ignore it. Because she had to hope that this would help with her restlessness. That it would give her something to pin her desires onto.

And children.

She looked at him hard.

"Even when you were in the dungeon, did you know that you would get out? Did you believe in it?"

"No," he said. "I didn't. I never let myself wonder about that, I never let myself carry concern about it.

I simply took the next breath." He paused for a moment. "Do you want children?"

"What would you do if I told you I didn't?"

"We both know that it might be too late for you to make such proclamations anyway. Given that we have not been careful."

"I know." She was silent for a breath. "I do want them. But I was just wondering… Since you never asked."

"But you do. And that's a good thing. Something that I can give you."

She thought it was strange, the way that he phrased that. Something that he could give her. She wondered what he meant by that. She wondered what exactly that meant to him.

"A foundation. And children."

And she was happy sitting there by his desk. Even though for some reason she hesitated to say it to him.

She didn't know why that was so difficult.

Maybe because this was nothing like she had thought. It certainly wasn't a sitcom life.

Except…

Maybe she had never wanted that classic two-story house. With a staircase that had a bend in it so the kids could run down the stairs and then jump over the railing at the end.

Maybe she had never wanted family dinners and big misunderstandings, and hijinks with pets.

Maybe what she had really wanted was to live in a house full of love.

Maybe that was what she really, really craved most of all.

That realization made her feel like something was pressing down on her chest.

Made her feel like she was carrying the weight of something impossible on her shoulders.

Because she was beginning to believe that she loved Riyaz. But as to whether or not he loved her, as to whether or not he could ever love anything. She simply didn't know. And she was too afraid to ask.

Then suddenly a man came through the door. A servant looked wide-eyed and terrified to be entering the Sheikh's domain.

"Ariel Hart has left. Cairo sent her away."

Riyaz went down into the dungeon. And there was his brother, laid out like it was his.

"What the hell are you doing?" he asked.

The voice came from the shadow. "I am seeing what it was like for you."

"Well. I still sleep down here. So you might ask before you enter."

"Why do you sleep down here?"

"Because you don't change immediately," said Riyaz. "I hate it here. And yet for many years it was the only place I saw. There is a safety to it. But it is captivity." He could hear his brother move toward him, sit down on the bench beside him. "But then. Everything is a cage of some kind. None of us are truly free."

"No," he said.

"I know that Ariel left. Why?"

"Because I told her to."

"I see. And why would you do that? You want to keep her."

"Look at where we are, Riyaz. We are in a dungeon. Do you really think it appropriate to keep a woman in the palace against her will? Even if it is in my bed and not a dungeon?"

"Did she say she didn't want to be with you?"

"No. But, she didn't have the choice to come here in the first place. Not now, and not all those years ago. She doesn't even know what she wants."

He laughed. "Is it her that doesn't know what she wants? Or is it you?"

"And what about you? You are keeping a woman prisoner as well."

"Have I expressed a moral difficulty with this?"

"I would think that you of all people would."

"Why?"

He had nothing to say to that. His brother simply didn't know… What was there to be said?

"Do you want her?" Riyaz asked him.

"Ariel? Of course. I have done everything to have her. I betrayed you. Again."

"What do you mean again?"

"You said that we should keep our demons to ourselves, Riyaz. But I think you should know about mine. I was in love with Ariel when we were children. And I used to sneak out with her. When we were fourteen we went out into the desert. And we were caught. I was. By her father. And he asked me a question… And I answered it. To keep myself from being in trouble. I gave him an easier way to get into the palace. I did not feel as if I could tell him no. Or he would… He would reveal what happened between myself and Ariel."

"So you're the reason they came into the palace."

"Yes," he said.

"That was a very stupid thing to do," said Riyaz.

His words were cold. His heart was cold. Everything in him was cold. Cairo had been the one. He'd been responsible. He'd let his guard down, and he'd been…out with Ariel. Betraying Riyaz, betraying Nazul.

And yet….

What could be done?

If Cairo had been wrong, so had their father been. To let that man into their home in the first place. To trust him, to make an alliance with him.

He felt…angry. He felt enraged, even. And yet… He would not react. What purpose would there be in it? He would lose his temper and he might harm his brother. He could not afford to let himself fully engage with this revelation.

And anyway, what good would it do? Nothing.

"It was," Cairo agreed.

"Fourteen-year-old boys are stupid," Riyaz said.

"Yes. And you were sixteen. And suffered greatly for my stupidity."

Years of stone walls flashed before his eyes. And yet he knew no matter what Cairo had or hadn't done, that would have been the outcome. He was a convenient scapegoat even now for the real villains, and while Riyaz had sharp and jagged feelings about all of this, he could not blame his brother.

Not wholly.

He might feel something angry or twisted up inside his chest, but in his mind he knew the truth.

"They were intent on killing the royal family, they would've done it somehow. Even if it'd been exploding a motorcade. It would've occurred. This was a neat and clean way to do it, but... They would've found a way."

"Are you trying to absolve me?"

He did not have that power. He couldn't pull the blood back from the stones of the palace. He could not offer absolution.

"No. Your actions led to that event. But you cannot control the intent of others. So yes, something that you did played a part in the way they were able to kill our parents and take me prisoner. But... I believe it would've happened either way. And perhaps we all would have been blown up."

"You can't know that."

"No. But you can't know otherwise."

"I don't understand," Cairo said. "Are you blaming me? Forgiving me?"

"I can do either. Here is one thing you learn with only yourself for company for a great number of years. The world turns regardless of your involvement in it. In the dark of night, you only have yourself. And the only way you can be rescued is if there someone out there who cares enough to do it. I can't absolve you. You have to absolve yourself. But you are the person who came for me. Whether you are blameless or not… That is something."

It wasn't a rousing speech of forgiveness. It was something deeper than that. It was something that Cairo could actually… Accept.

Neither of them was perfect. But they were here together in the dark. He had come for Riyaz when Riyaz needed him. And now Riyaz had come for him. And perhaps they could never make fair the things that were unfair. And perhaps they could never make whole the things that were broken.

And perhaps he could never be redeemed.

But maybe… Maybe he could be loved. Just as he was anyway. Because wasn't that what Riyaz was giving him? Not absolution, and not blame. Just acceptance.

"I have to go to her," he said.

"Of course you do," said Riyaz.

"I'm not taking her prisoner."

"I wouldn't care if you were."

"Yes. I know."

He wouldn't care if Cairo was taking her prisoner, because he supposed that was what he had done to Brianna. He had to be honest about that. He had not initially given her a choice, and while she had said yes eventually, he still felt…

He still knew that he was denying her that dream she'd always had.

That normal life.

He had claimed her in the desert, whether she'd wanted to be claimed or not. He had not asked. Though in the end, she had said yes. And he had offered her a foundation. So there was that.

He didn't know what he felt about what Cairo had said. That he was the one who had given the men the keys to the palace. But he was the reason Riyaz had been locked away. That their mother was dead.

But he didn't have it in him to demonize his brother. Not in the least. He simply didn't have the will.

But it left him feeling something he couldn't quite put a finger on. There was something burning inside of him. Some rage. But it was a fruitless rage.

Cairo was his last living family member. There was nothing… There was nothing.

"Get your woman," said Riyaz.

And Cairo did. He left.

As it should be.

But Riyaz simply had his feelings. His own flashbacks to that time.

Riyaz had loved his mother.

His father.

Cairo had loved Ariel. And it had made him make a foolish mistake, but he had been just a boy.

He had only been a boy. What was there to condemn?

He felt like something violent had grabbed a hold of him and shaken him.

He felt numb. Or perhaps it wasn't numbness, but a dawning realization. A peeling back of all the pain and grief that echoed in his soul.

Grim acceptance had kept him alive. Brianna did say he was grim.

The belief he was keeping himself alive all those years by holding it at bay.

The belief he was protecting Brianna by holding his emotions back. That he could not love, because he could not open up the depths of himself in that way and put her at risk.

But there, with his soul scraped raw, and his anger, his pain, at Cairo, at his father, at the men who had done these things…

The memory of his mother.

It was not blind anger that drove him now, but grief. For the way his family had been destroyed and the burden they all carried as a result and it was too heavy.

He could not hold any more.

He could not care for anyone. It would be too costly.

He was not protecting her.

He was protecting him.

He was not a hero.
He was a prisoner.
He did not leave the dungeon.

CHAPTER ELEVEN

BRIANNA LOOKED EVERYWHERE for Riyaz. Except the dungeon. He didn't normally go down there at this time. And yet… There was something that had made her want to check. So she crept down there. And there he was. Sitting in the darkness.

"Riyaz? What's going on?"

"I found Cairo down here. I sent him after Ariel."

"That was very good of you."

"Why?"

Brianna looked away. "I know it was complicated because she was your…"

He gripped her chin and turned her head to face him, forcing her to meet his eyes. "I don't want her." The flame she saw there burned, and it took him a full minute to release his hold on her. "I do not want her in the least. It was not hard at all. It was nothing."

"What's the matter?"

"Cairo… He told me something. He is the reason that those men were able to get into the palace. He gave information to Ariel's father, because he trusted the man. And he was afraid that he and Ariel would get in trouble for being outside the palace. They were children."

"Oh, Riyaz. That must be... Devastating."

He looked up at her. "Why should it be? My brother was a child. He meant nothing by it. He was no more wrong for trusting that man than my father was."

But there was tension there. Something that he wasn't quite telling her.

"Riyaz... Speak to me."

"There is nothing to say."

"Well, would you at least come upstairs for dinner?"

"I... I could."

"Come with me. I don't think you should be alone. I'm also happy to bring something down here. If that's what you want."

"No. We will go upstairs."

She could feel erratic energy coming off of him. And she didn't know what it was. She couldn't quite put a finger on it. She wasn't sure what he was thinking or how... Black his mood was. There was a roast turkey for dinner. And the spread on the table was lovely. Riyaz did not observe any of his learned manners when he sat down, throwing the chair out behind him, and sitting heavily.

"It's all right if you're angry," she said, dishing herself some turkey, and adding some jeweled couscous to her plate.

"I'm not angry. Everybody trusted Ariel's father. All of the men in my family. Why should that make me angry? It simply is. Cairo is no less than my father."

"Is that honestly how you feel?"

"It doesn't matter what I feel. Feelings are not the facts of the situation."

"Or maybe it does matter what you feel, Riyaz. Maybe it does."

"He is my brother," he said. "He is my brother, and I will not condemn him."

"You don't have to condemn him to feel something."

"Enough," he said. He began to put food on his plate. "I am the Sheikh. Cairo is my brother. There is no scope…"

"Who cares about the scope? You're right. Why don't we have honesty between us for a moment. Wildness. Who cares if you're the Sheikh? Who cares if I'm supposed to civilize you?" She wanted love. She recognized that now. She understood it. For what it was.

"Be honest about what you feel. Because it's the only way that you're actually going to move forward from any of this."

"Moving forward. This is not pop psychology. This is my life. This is a kingdom."

"Right here, with me, this is just… Real. This is just feelings. Please. Riyaz, tell me what that made you feel."

"It makes me feel… Makes me feel as if my mother's blood is on his hands. And he… He went free. He ran away, didn't he?" Riyaz looked up at her, his dark eyes blazing. "He ran away from this. From us. He's been free. All this time. Earning money and making the life that he wanted, and… Hell. He's had whatever he's wanted. All the women he's wanted."

Pain lanced her chest. "Is that what you need? Do you need more women…? Do you need…?"

"No," he said darkly. "I don't need more women. I can have a harem if I want to. I am the Sheikh. I can do whatever I want. I… It doesn't matter."

"What is it that's upsetting you?"

"I was in a dungeon. In the darkness. I'm not the one who caused it. Why was I the one who was punished? Why were we punished?"

"I don't know," she said. "I don't know I…"

"This is when you tell me that Cairo would feel terrible about all of this. Because he's a good man. He's your friend."

"He is my friend. But you're my fiancé. And I don't need to defend him. He's your brother. You love him. That doesn't mean that you can't be angry. That doesn't mean that you can't feel something about the fact that… That his mistake led to this. He has had sixteen years to have feelings about it. You can have feelings. Why shouldn't you? Why shouldn't you have feelings?"

"They mean nothing. They mean nothing. All you

can do when you're prisoner is simply survive. It is all you have."

"Do you feel like a prisoner? Are you still just a prisoner here?"

He looked away. "None of it matters."

Oh, how she hated this. The way that they were both bound up here. In duty. In love. Duty for him. Love for her.

"I do not need other women," he said, his voice suddenly hard. "I need you."

And she wanted to be enough for him. She wanted to be everything.

She wanted to find a way to restore everything that they had lost. "Then you can have me."

"Do you not wish to have your dinner?" he asked. There was a vague sneer in his voice, and it surprised her. Riyaz was many things, but rarely unkind. Not to her. And she thought that perhaps this was a reflection of something else.

He's in pain.

"I don't need anything but you," she said. "Believe me. All I need is you."

He growled, and reached across the space, pulling her from her chair and bringing her over onto his. "Why would I need any other woman when I have you? Most beautiful of women. Whenever I desire. Because you are mine. You are going to be my wife."

"Yes," she said. "The wedding is being planned."

"Yes," he said, his voice rough.

There was something fractured in him now. Something on the verge of shattering entirely.

And she wanted to hold them together. Desperately.

And she would show him that she was strong enough. She was.

She was not the girl that she had been, afraid. Forced into a life she didn't want. She was not the woman who had escaped. Who had sought to fit in to her surroundings. Who had tried to blend in seamlessly. This woman who had been so afraid that people would identify that she was different.

But she was happy to be different. She was happy to be herself. Brianna Whitman. A woman strong enough for this man. A woman who could help him navigate the world as he needed to, but let him be who he was when they were together.

"There need be no rules between us," she said. "Those rules are for dignitaries. Sit how you want. Eat how you want. Be how you want. Be angry if you want to be angry. You never have to hide yourself for me," she said.

It was an echo of the time they had shared out of the fountain. When passion had welled up between them and he had demanded that they embrace their wildness. But this was something more. Something deeper.

They did not need to perform for one another. Not ever. They did not need to play parts. She was not a foreign diplomat, and he was not a teacher at a boarding school that she was trying to impress. They were for each other. And yes, maybe parts of the world were a prison. Performances that you had to engage in. But the two of them never would be. Not ever.

She tore his shirt open.

"In the dining room?"

"Don't tell me that's not what you were thinking," she said.

He tore her top from her head, and then began to push her skirt up to her hips. And then he swept her panties to the side and began to stroke her there, between her thighs. She put her hand over his cloth-covered arousal, and he groaned. Then she began to open up the closure on his pants. She freed him, arching her hips forward and sinking down slowly onto his arousal. He filled her. Perfectly. Absolutely. They weren't generally fast like this. He preferred to take their time and feast on one another.

She loved that about him.

She knew that he took exceptional care with her body because there had been no other women before her, so he was never riding on empty experience. Never enacting moves that he had done before. It was all about her. It was all about what it made her feel. All about what she wanted. And that made her feel… Exceptionally good. It made her feel special. But this was something she needed. Fast. Furious. Him. Always him.

She cried out with pleasure as she began to ride him. As he clutched her hips, hard and strong, bringing her up and down over his body. She let her head fall back, a scream escaping her lips. "I love you," she said.

And that was when everything stopped. Everything. At first she thought he meant to leave her body, but then he roared, his climax shaking them both. And he clung to her, his heart pounding in his chest as he stroked her hair.

"I love you," she whispered.

"No," he said. "You do not say that."

But he didn't release his hold on her. "Why not?"

"Because. It is not for me. I do not like the words."

"Riyaz…"

"Let us go to bed."

And that was when he picked her up, and much to her great surprise, he propelled them both not to the dungeon, but upstairs. He laid her down on the bed and he kissed her. And it reminded her so much of their first time together. Something sweet. Something for the two of them. But inside she was breaking.

It wasn't even that he hadn't said he loved her in return. It was his outright rejection of her love.

It was that he wouldn't even let her say it. That he wouldn't accept it. It just felt wrong. Why wouldn't he let her love him?

But then he was kissing her again. Trailing a path of fire down her neck, down to her breast, and she found it difficult to think. Because he was too much. And not enough all at once. Because she was caught in the reality of the situation. Of this life that she was choosing.

Because love was what made the family, and if he couldn't say it… If he couldn't even accept it… Then what did that mean?

Except she couldn't think, because the alternative was a life without this. A life without him.

And it wasn't as if you were given the option anyway.

No. She supposed that she hadn't been given that option.

But then he was in her again, and she just wanted to exist in that moment. In that space. Where they were together. Where they were one. Where she hadn't said that she loved him and he hadn't rejected it. Because it felt better to not know. It felt better to leave it as an open and wonderful possibility, rather than have it closed down as something that could never be.

In the end she wondered what did it matter. If she could say that she loved him, if he could accept it. So long as she did. Wasn't that the most right thing? Wasn't that the most real? Wasn't that the most important thing?

And he took her to the heights again. And she decided that maybe that was the thing. They had these heights. And it didn't matter what they were called.

There was no laugh track on this. No canned responses from the audience to let her know how to feel. There was simply… There was simply all of this.

And it was good.

It was good.

This was the life she chose.

It might not be normal or perfect.

But it was hers.

And much to her surprise, he held her against his body, and they went to sleep.

CHAPTER TWELVE

WHEN HE WOKE UP, there was violence coursing through his veins. Black heat and fire, and the terror of what was to come.

And somewhere, in all of that, something cut through.

I love you.

I love you.

And he looked down and saw his mother, broken and bleeding on the floor.

I love you.

That was the last time he had heard those words. That was the last time. And it tore at him. It made him feel like his chest was nothing more than a bloody wound. It made him feel like nothing in his body was his own.

Except for the pain. The pain was his.

The loss was his.

And in that vision he saw his brother, he saw his father.

And he turned on them.

How dare you!

How dare you trust the wrong people. Look at what you've done. Look at what you've done to her.

There was pain in his chest and there was nowhere for it to go. There was nothing. Because then he was in a dungeon, and he could not afford to show weakness to his captors. He could give them nothing. He could show no pain. He could never let them know.

No. He could never let them know. And so he pushed everything down. The grief. The pain. The rage.

But it didn't work. The rage still bubbled over.

He was not in control at all anymore. The years of it melting away as if it had never been.

It was as he'd always known.

Love made him so very weak. Love made it so he could not hold back the tide of pain that lived in his soul.

And he grabbed something, something heavy, and he threw it toward the part of the room he saw his father and brother in.

But then dimly, he heard a voice. The same voice that had said I love you. Not his mother's.

"Riyaz. Please. Please."

And he realized it was her. And he wasn't back with his parents. He wasn't back in that day. In that space. He was with Brianna.

She had said that she loved him.

His father had failed a woman who loved him. His brother had likewise failed a woman who loved him.

Riyaz had not. Not yet. But it was in his blood, his DNA.

You already have failed her.

You've taken her prisoner.

He was holding her in that cell with him, for he had concluded he was still a prisoner. Of all that had come before. Of all the pain and grief and death, and now she was here with him, instead of in that normal, beautiful house she wanted.

He had proven that in fact he was his brother.

He had felt all that simmering rage at Cairo for his weakness. For the lie that he had bought into. For his cowardice.

He was keeping her prisoner. He was no better than Cairo. He was no better than the men who held him captive.

How was he any different? He might not have spilled any blood, but he was failing a woman who loved him. A woman who should not love him.

For he had given her no reason to. He had done nothing but treat her with disrespect. He had done nothing but treat her as if she was a coup.

And somewhere in the darkness, the haze cleared.

And he was fully in the moment. And Brianna's hands were on him. She was comforting him. She was comforting him as she had done all these times.

And what had he given her?

He had sought to give her pleasure. He had known it would not be enough.

He had sought to give her…

He had not tried very hard.

Normal.

She wanted normal. She had told him exactly what she wanted, and he had not listened.

She had told him that what she wanted was to have that life that she saw on TV. Those family dinners, and what had he given her? Cold meals at a banquet table, and then he had brought her onto his lap and had her right there where anyone could've walked in. It was not what he had promised.

And he would release her now. He had to.

He could not see a way to let himself out of this cell, for he could not endure all of this…feeling.

But he did not have to keep her in it as well.

But in that moment, he faltered. In that moment, he reached for the light, because he wished to see her clearly.

She was naked, standing before him unashamed and unafraid. She had given him her body. She had given him some measure of peace.

And he had done what? Grown her character? Tested her strength? She did not deserve that.

"Brianna," he said. "I want you to go."

"Riyaz, we've been through this. I'm not afraid of you. And I can handle this."

"I don't mean out of my room. I mean away from the palace. I want you to go back to New York. Go back to your town house. Sell it. Buy a house in a neighborhood. I told you that your dreams were not enough. But that was wrong. What you want… It matters. I took it from you. Your choice. I will not do that. Not anymore. I cannot do that."

"Riyaz," she said. "Didn't you hear me when I said that I loved you?"

"Yes. But I am not able to receive it. And loving me denies you of the very thing you want most."

"No," she said. "It's just… It's what I thought I wanted. But I realized something. Normal doesn't mean anything. What I was missing in my family home was love." She shook her head. "That's what I want. I just want love."

"And I cannot give it to you. Don't you see? I grew up in a home where there was plenty of love. It didn't keep her safe. Remember? It doesn't keep you safe. Beth can still die. Remember *Little Women*?"

"This isn't Civil War–era America. And you aren't going to get scarlet fever."

"But it won't protect you. That's what I'm telling you. It will not protect you from what might befall you. But that normal life? That will protect you."

"Tell me why. Tell me why you don't think you can love me."

"Aside from the sixteen years spent in a dungeon? Many reasons. But I cannot… it's my mother's face I see. Dying. Bleeding. They are not good words for me. And I can't…" The pain was too much, and the closer he got to her…

The closer he got to losing every last shred of protection he'd placed around his soul.

"Riyaz…"

"I will fail you. I have failed you. But I won't again. You will go. And you will not come back."

"Riyaz," she said, looking shocked.

And he felt a shard of glass work its way up through his chest.

"I'm the Sheikh. And I have spoken."

CHAPTER THIRTEEN

SHE WAS FROZEN. Ashamedly paralyzed. And it lasted until the sleek private jet touched down in New York. Until she was back on American soil, feeling like a foreigner in her own country. In her own skin. In every way.

Every time she breathed it was like shards of glass being ground deeper and deeper into her chest. And she had to ask herself... Why? Why had she gone so easily? Why had she walked away from the life that she had chosen?

She had been rescued before. This wasn't the same. She didn't need to be rescued from Riyaz, and yet...

She knew why she had gone. Right then, she knew why. She had gone because he needed her to.

He needed to set her free. Or maybe he needed to set himself free. And in the end, the thing that made her laugh was... She was willing to do that. To walk away because he might need a reprieve.

She would not become his dungeon. Even though

that might be his motivation for letting her go… She wouldn't be that for him either. She refused.

He had precious little choice in his life.

And if he asked her to go… If he said he didn't want to hear that she loved him…

There were two things, she knew it. There was something in him that was afraid to be too strong, afraid that he might be overwhelming her with force. And something else in him that scared him perhaps even more. Something that he thought might be too weak. The kind of weakness that he saw in his brother, even though he loved him. The kind of weakness he saw in his father, even though he loved him.

And it was all twisted up in that haunting last thing his mother had said to him. He was a man who simply didn't trust. Not the world. Not himself. And how could she ask him to?

She didn't have an answer. So she just stumbled into her town house and looked around. It was a nice place, because of course Cairo would never have bought her a home that wasn't nice. But there was also something incredibly… Normal about it. It was one of the things that she had liked. Right away. The lightly flowered wallpaper, the little breakfast nook in the corner.

It usually made her happy.

But unfortunately, she had been right. The thing that made those families enviable was their love. The thing that made those lovely, normal houses an object of desire was the love within the walls, not the walls themselves.

She had been totally cut off from her family.

She'd had to cut herself off from them, and she had to conform to the outside world. And only with Riyaz had she really felt free.

Maybe there was another lesson in there as well. That you could be normal, or you could be free. But you couldn't be both.

Her chest ached. And she wished she had a friend. One other than Cairo. And then she remembered that she did.

Hesitantly, she decided to call Ariel, whose number she had put in her phone a week or so ago.

"Hello?" She breathed out heavily. "Thank God, Brianna. I was worried."

"I just made it back to New York."

"We're trying to keep word from spreading about the canceled wedding. Just... Just in case."

Brianna looked at the clock on the wall. A very normal-looking clock. Except for who had clocks on the wall anymore? But she had thought that it made a nice accessory. It was a set, this place. She had never really noticed it before.

And owed to the kind of normalcy that she had long thought she needed in order to feel whole.

"I don't think he wants me to come back. He... He set me free. And he told me that I wasn't supposed to come back."

"Cairo tried that with me," said Ariel. "He told me

that I hadn't chosen to be married to him. He told me that I needed to be free. To make my own choices."

"So they're the same man, just in a slightly different configuration of trauma."

"Yes. And they did both take us without permission."

She waved a hand even though Ariel wasn't there to see it. "Semantics. I think it's pretty apparent we both want to stay."

"Riyaz was a man in a dungeon, Brianna. I think he couldn't stand the thought of you feeling locked away also."

"I think he's a man afraid of being locked in the dungeon by his feelings for me. That's what I think."

There was a long pause. "Maybe you have a point."

"Did Cairo talk to you? About the fact that he feels responsible for what happened at the palace?"

"Yes. He said Riyaz was very calm."

"He was. He almost didn't react at all. But he's broken by it. And I'm afraid… Actually, I'm afraid the real issue is he doesn't want to step outside the dungeon. He doesn't want to be too angry. He doesn't want to want too much. He doesn't want to feel too much. He doesn't want to ever love anything that can be taken from him." And for a moment, she just felt overwhelmed. By everything that he needed. By everything she wanted to do for him.

And the limits of what she would be able to.

She was just a girl who had been playing the part of somebody who understood normal.

You understand him. You want to. Maybe that's what matters.

"What should I do? I love him. But he already has to do so much for so many people. He has to be the ruler of his country. And where does that leave him? Where does that leave him and what choice does he have in anything?"

"He's going to have to step out of the dungeon," she said. "The dungeon in his mind. More than anything else. He's going to have to… He has to decide."

"And if he can't?" Brianna asked.

"He will," said Ariel.

"Why do you think that?"

"Because I know his brother very well. And because I know how those men love. He might not be able to tell you that he loves you, Brianna, but he does. I'm certain of it."

"Should I come back?"

"Give it a few days," said Ariel. "I think my husband is going to return the favor that he owes your fiancée."

"What favor is that?"

"You know, even when Cairo confessed to Riyaz that it was his fault the palace had been taken… He encouraged Cairo to go back to me. To have me. He could recognize when something is good for someone else. I just think he's having difficulty accepting it for himself. Let Cairo help. And trust… Trust that Riyaz is strong enough to break the chains."

CHAPTER FOURTEEN

RIYAZ HAD NOT felt pain like this since his parents' deaths. On the nights when he had flashed back to their deaths, it was the closest. That was what it was to wake up without Brianna in the palace. Pain. Like a death. It was he who was standing at the top of the stairs, looking down into the dungeon, when he heard footsteps behind him.

"So here we are in a very similar position to what we were in only a couple of weeks ago," said his brother, Cairo, from behind.

"Yes."

"You sent her away."

"I had to. I was forcing her to stay with me when I knew that she wanted something else. You know what you saved Brianna from. You know that her father was going to traffic her. He was a criminal. How can I hold her captive?"

"Well, you could. But you aren't. Because you're a decent person."

"Yes, I am. At least, I am trying to be."

"The thing is, though, eventually, you have to listen to what she wants. She's in love with you?"

"She said she was. But I…"

"You're angry with me, aren't you?"

"Of course not. What you told me has nothing to do with this."

"I think you're lying, my brother. I think you're angry with me. You were very calm. When I told you."

"What is the alternative?"

"Throw some fists. Rage. For God's sake. You're a monster that has been kept in a dungeon for sixteen years, and you can't pull together a little bit of barbarian fury?"

"I don't want to," he said. "What is the point of it? I never raged. I never… I never cried. Nothing. Because what would the point be? Everyone was dead and I was in chains."

"Yes," he said. "Everyone was dead and you were in chains, so what was the point? And yet you have feelings about it. You are not in a dungeon anymore. You're allowed to have feelings."

And suddenly, a nameless rage inside of him boiled over and he grabbed his brother by the throat and pinned him to the wall. "Well, why did you tell him? Why did you tell them how to get into the palace?"

"Because I was foolish. I made a mistake."

"Yes, you did," said Riyaz. "Yes, you did."

"You're allowed to be angry."

"I am," said Riyaz, pounding his fist hard against the stone wall. "I am furious. But Father... He should've known. He should never have trusted him. He should never have put you in that position. Or me. And Mother... He was supposed to protect her."

"Yes," Cairo said. "He was. He didn't. She paid the consequences for that. So did you."

"So did he," said Riyaz. "And this rage is pointless. Because it solves nothing and it brings no one back. Because... The only blame that is to be laid is on the people who... The people who destroyed us. The people who destroyed our family. Our country. Me."

"You're not destroyed," said Cairo. "If I'm not destroyed, then neither are you. I tried. In the back of my mind I knew I needed to come back, I needed to save you. And in the meantime, I tried to self-destruct with excess. I figured even if I limped back here, freed you, but was little more than a shadow of myself, it would all be fine. But I found something better. I found something better than self-destruction. I found love."

Riyaz closed his eyes. "But..." Everything felt painful. Sharp. But suddenly, just suddenly, he realized he didn't hate the words *I love you*. He craved them. It was just that his heart, which had been frozen solid out of the need to survive, hadn't been able to tell the difference. Between a desperate desire and a deeper unrelenting fear. Because they were the same. Because wanting anything had been his enemy. And he felt… It was as if truth was pouring from his chest like blood. And he could scarcely manage it all. He could scarcely understand himself. "I need to go," he said.

"All right. If you need to hit me…"

"I don't," said Riyaz.

Because it was as if that blockade of emotions was suddenly becoming clear. What started as anger, the kind that sent him on blind rages when he had those flashbacks, the kind that had overtaken him just now… They were deeper. And they were more. It was grief. The grief he had never been allowed to have.

And he knew he could have no good thing without allowing the pain out as well.

And because he could, he opened the doors to the palace and he ran. Into the desert, he ran as far as his legs would take him. Because he was free. And then he sank to his knees and he cried out at the unfeeling sky. And a sob tore itself free from his chest, tears falling from his eyes. The tears he had never allowed himself to shed. Sixteen years of them. For the loss of his mother. The loss of his father. The loss of sixteen years of his life.

For all that had been taken from him, all of it. Until he had poured out the unrelenting grief onto the sand.

Until he was emptied of it. These years of pain. All of them.

But there was still something there, a restlessness. A memory.

The love he used to have for his family. And now that the rawness of grief had been removed... That love was still there. But where would it go? And that created a deep sadness within him.

For her. For them.

He wanted to hear that he was loved again. He looked at the sky again, and a hawk sliced through the pale blue. And he did not think the sky was so unfeeling after all.

She was trying to do what Ariel said. She was trying to wait. And wait well.

But it was difficult. But she had to trust... She knew what had passed between them. What had passed between their bodies, whether or not he had been ready to admit what had passed between their souls. And she believed that it was love.

Still, she had put the town house up for sale. And where she would go after, she didn't know. Would it be a cul-de-sac? She hoped not. She would try the palace first. But there was no way to know for sure.

She shut the door behind her one last time and turned the lock. And then she put her hands in her coat pockets and began to walk down the street.

"Brianna."

It was his voice. He said her name in a way only he could. As if he was tasting it. As if it was something special and new. Something he had never tried before.

"You're here," she said.

She looked at him, backed by the city. By sky-scrapers, all concrete and glass.

He was in New York. He was out of the dungeon.

"Riyaz…"

"Cairo is managing things in my stead. And I am… I am here."

"You are."

"Maybe I should play tourist."

"You? A tourist?"

"Why not?" he asked. "I'm here."

"Well, I can't invite you over. I did just…sell the town house. I have a room at a hotel until I decide where to go next. I got rid of all my things."

"And why is that?"

"I was really hoping that you would come. That's why."

"I also have a hotel reservation. It might be nicer than yours."

"Probably. Though, hotels have beds, not jail cells."

"I would think that in New York you could find one with a jail cell."

She laughed. "Was that a joke?"

"It was. I read about many of these places. I can't wait to see them. With you. I hope you understand I mean with you. Because you're why I'm here. I love you, *habibti*. Brianna. And it is not because you are the first woman. It is that you are the only woman. The only one for me. I had to… Feel. Everything.

The anger. The grief. Sorrow. So that I could begin to feel the joy. I had to trust that it would not be taken away from me, and only then was I able to see. I did not hate love. I craved it. But when you're in a place of deprivation, wanting is the enemy. So I trained myself not to want. And eventually trained myself to believe all of that was bad. But I want cake. And sunshine and you. I said that my destiny was to rule Nazul. That it was part of me. My blood. But I realize now you are entangled in that destiny. If it took a coup, imprisonment, your awful father, and Cairo, for the two of us to meet, then I will call it all filled with meaning. You take tragedy that could be pointless and make it into something… It in and of itself is not beautiful, you understand, but it has made me into a man who has you. And for that I will be grateful. For that, I can leave the past behind."

"I understand. I thought that I wanted normal. I just wanted to be loved. I wanted to love someone. And I do."

"And I love you."

"And I have my dream. Exactly the way that I always wanted."

He frowned. "I'm not living in a cul-de-sac."

She had to laugh at the expression his face. "I don't dream of cul-de-sacs," she said. "I only dream of you."

The slow grin that cut across his taciturn face was like seeing the sun for the first time. "Good. Then let's go sightseeing."

He took her hand in his, like he was her boyfriend and they were about to set out on a very normal date. Not like he was a sheikh, and she his future sheikha. Not like she had been a prisoner in her own home growing up, and he had been a literal prisoner of a dungeon.

But just as they were.

Just whole, and together.

"What do you want to see?" she asked.

He thought for a moment. "Whatever we want."

And so they did. Because they were free. And they were in love.

EPILOGUE

THE GRAND AFFAIR of their wedding was storied. Written about in publications all over the world. A fairy tale. And on their wedding night, she got to give her husband another surprise.

"Where else would you like to go?" he said. "The wonderful thing about technology is so much ruling of a country can be done from other locations."

She had created a monster. Riyaz did not just like to go outside. He liked to hike. He liked to see the world. Everything that he had ever read about. They had stayed in the rather run-down diner in New York City for longer than she would've liked because he was so entranced by the atmosphere, and how it was exactly as described in a spy novel he'd read.

He was a menace. And she loved him. And she realized that... She was actually getting to live many lives with him. Because they both got to live their dreams with each other.

"Well, that would be a good idea. And we do need to get more flying in before..."

"Before what?"

"They don't like you to fly too late in your pregnancy."

He stood up off the bed. "Really?"

"Yes."

And then he dropped to his knees, and put his hand on her stomach. He looked up at her, his dark eyes filled with emotion. "Brianna, there was a time in my life when I had nothing but darkness. Nothing but despair. And a dungeon. And you have given me the world. You made me the Sheikh. A man. Husband. Now father. What have I given you?"

She leaned in and kissed him. "Everything that I ever wanted."

* * * * *

#4145 CHRISTMAS BABY WITH HER ULTRA-RICH BOSS
by Michelle Smart

Ice hotel manager Lena Weir's job means the world to her. So succumbing to temptation for one night with her boss, Konstantinos Siopis, was reckless—but oh-so-irresistible. Except their passion left her carrying a most unprofessional consequence... This Christmas, she's expecting the billionaire's heir!

#4146 CONTRACTED AS THE ITALIAN'S BRIDE
by Julia James

Becoming Dante Cavelli's convenient bride is the answer to waitress Connie Weston's financial troubles. For the first time, she can focus on herself, and her resulting confidence captivates Dante, leading to an attraction that may cause them to violate the terms of their on-paper union...

#4147 PREGNANT AND STOLEN BY THE TYCOON
by Maya Blake

Tech genius Genie Merchant will only sell the algorithm she's spent years perfecting to a worthy buyer. When notoriously ruthless Severino Valente makes an offer, their off-the-charts chemistry means she'll entertain it...if he'll give her the baby she wants more than anything!

#4148 TWELVE NIGHTS IN THE PRINCE'S BED
by Clare Connelly

The last thing soon-to-be king Adrastros can afford is a scandal. When photos of his forbidden tryst with Poppy Henderson are sold to the press, he must save both of their reputations...by convincing the world that their passion was the start of a festive royal romance!

HPCNMRA0923

#4149 THE CHRISTMAS THE GREEK CLAIMED HER
From Destitute to Diamonds
by Millie Adams
Maren Hargreave always dreamed of being a princess. When she wins a castle and a crown in a poker game, she's convinced she's found her hard-earned happily-ever-after. But she hadn't realized that in claiming her prize, she's also *marrying* intoxicating billionaire Acastus Diakos!

#4150 HIRED FOR THE BILLIONAIRE'S SECRET SON
by Joss Wood
This summer will be Olivia Cooper's last as a nanny. So she knows that she can't allow herself to get attached to single father Bo Sørenson. Her impending departure *should* make it easier to ignore the billionaire's incendiary gaze...but it only makes it harder to ignore their heat!

#4151 HIS ASSISTANT'S NEW YORK AWAKENING
by Emmy Grayson
Temporary assistant Evolet Grey has precisely the skills and experience needed to help Damon Bradford win the biggest contract in his company's history. But the innocent is also distractingly attractive and testing the iron grip the Manhattan CEO *always* has on his self-control...

#4152 THE FORBIDDEN PRINCESS HE CRAVES
by Lorraine Hall
Sent to claim Elsebet as his brother's wife, Danil Laurentius certainly didn't expect an accident to leave him stranded with the captivating princess. And as she tends to his injuries, the ever-intensifying attraction between them makes him long for the impossible... He wants to claim innocent Elsebet for himself!

YOU CAN FIND MORE INFORMATION ON UPCOMING HARLEQUIN TITLES, FREE EXCERPTS AND MORE AT HARLEQUIN.COM.

HPCNMRB0923

Get 3 FREE REWARDS!

We'll send you 2 FREE Books plus a FREE Mystery Gift.

FREE
Value Over
$20

Both the **Harlequin® Desire** and **Harlequin Presents®** series feature compelling
novels filled with passion, sensuality and intriguing scandals.

HARLEQUIN
PLUS

Try the best multimedia
subscription service for romance
readers like you!

Read, Watch and Play.

Experience the easiest way to get
the romance content you crave.

Start your **FREE TRIAL** at
<u>www.harlequinplus.com/freetrial</u>.